*When Bryant spoke, his voice
had lost its hard note of despair.*

"How do you do that, Deborah? How do you make me hope again?" His hand cupped her face. "How do you make me want?"

Want? It felt more like an ache. He stirred feelings she hadn't experienced in years, created needs she couldn't name.

But he'd promised her a year, then he'd leave town. With her heart hammering against her ribs, she broke away.

Dear Reader,

This month, Silhouette Romance presents an exciting new FABULOUS FATHER from Val Whisenand. Clay Ellis is *A Father Betrayed*—surprised to learn he has a child and has been deceived by the woman he'd always loved.

Long Lost Husband is a dramatic new romance from favorite author Joleen Daniels. Andrea Ballanger thought her ex-husband, Travis Hunter, had been killed in the line of duty. But then she learned Travis was very much alive....

Bachelor at the Wedding continues Sandra Steffen's heartwarming WEDDING WAGER series about three brothers who vow they'll never say "I do." This month, Kyle Harris loses the bet—and his heart—when he catches the wedding garter and falls for would-be bride Clarissa Cohagan.

Rounding out the month, you'll find love and laughter as a determined single mom tries to make herself over completely—much to the dismay of the man who loves her—in Terry Essig's *Hardheaded Woman*. In *The Baby Wish*, Myrna Mackenzie tells the touching story of a woman who longs to be a mother. Too bad her handsome boss has given up on family life—or so he thought.

And visit Sterling, Montana, for a delightful tale from Kara Larkin. There's a new doctor in town, and though he isn't planning on staying, pretty Deborah Pingree hopes he'll make some *Home Ties*.

Until next month, happy reading!

Anne Canadeo
Senior Editor
Silhouette Romance

Please address questions and book requests to:
Silhouette Reader Service
U.S.: 3010 Walden Ave., P.O. Box 1325, Buffalo, NY 14269
Canadian: P.O. Box 609, Fort Erie, Ont. L2A 5X3

HOME TIES

Kara Larkin

ROMANCE™
Published by Silhouette Books
America's Publisher of Contemporary Romance

To Steve—
it takes a true hero
to support someone else's dream

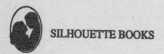 SILHOUETTE BOOKS

ISBN 0-373-19047-6

HOME TIES

KARA LARKIN

likes to accumulate experience points in the game of life. Going to new places and meeting new people provide a rich background for her stories. She loves her husband, is in awe of her children and treasures her friends. In addition to writing romance novels, she gardens, bicycles and teaches fiction writing.

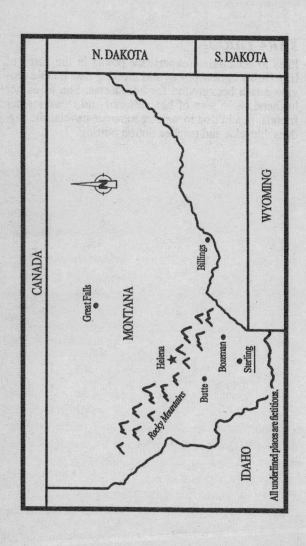

All underlined places are fictitious.

Chapter One

"This is the last one." Deborah Pingree drove a nail into the underside of the eaves, her heart pounding as loudly as the hammer. "Do you have the end of the sheet?" she called to Ann. "Okay, let's roll it up."

With the sheet secure, she threw the ball of twine to Lane and slid to the ground. Ann jumped off the porch railing and grabbed one side of the ladder to help Deborah take it down.

Because both Deborah's daughters worked quickly and well, the job had gone without a hitch. Now, the sooner they left their next-door neighbor's yard the better. Even the security provided by the half-light of dusk wouldn't save them from gossip if someone drove by. In a town as small as Sterling, rumor traveled fast, evolving in shape and texture along the way. If this story took flight, who knew what variation of it the new doctor would hear?

Whether from nerves or the chill of evening, Deborah shivered. It had been a particularly warm day for April in Montana, but now the breezes of evening stirred through the trees.

"Are you sure it will work, Mom?" Lane asked.

"Of course." Grinning, Deborah gave the girl's ponytail a quick tug. "My ideas always work."

"Come on, let's get this finished," Ann prodded.

Quickly, Deborah directed her daughters as they arranged the trip line so it ran down the porch's support post and across the lawn to the driveway. They hooked it around a rock, ran it at bumper height across the drive and tied it to a bush. While the girls gathered tools and twine, Deborah picked up the ladder. Suddenly the low hum of a car's engine cut through the rural silence.

Exchanging glances and dragging their tools along, all three dived behind the bushes lining the irrigation ditch that ran parallel to the driveway.

"What if it's them?" Lane whispered urgently.

"They won't be here until day after tomorrow." Even knowing she couldn't possibly be overheard, Deborah kept her voice low and surveyed the area to see if they'd left anything incriminating behind.

Ann laughed. "Even if it is, they can't hear you from here."

"Whoever it is, we'd still better stay down," Deborah cautioned.

When the car slowed to turn into the driveway, three bodies flattened against the ground.

"It *is* them," Lane said.

Ann gave her sister a quelling look. "Well, I hope it's not somebody else. All that work for nothing!"

The car hit the trip line and the white sheet unfurled from the eaves of the house, with HEY DOC! WELCOME TO STERLING printed in huge, fluorescent green letters that gleamed in the car's headlights.

Gravel crunched as the car jerked to a stop.

"Oh, Lord, it's them for sure," Deborah muttered, glad she'd gotten the house ready for them well in advance. "Nobody around here drives a car like that. I hope he's got a sense of humor."

She tried to discern the features of the driver when he got out of the car. From her distorted perspective, he seemed taller than average. He wore casual slacks and an elegant knit shirt that hugged his chest—not exactly local dress. In the fading light, his hair might be any color, light brown or blond or gray, but it had obviously been professionally styled. He didn't smile when his eyes passed over the message hanging across the porch.

The passenger door opened, and the boy who climbed out appeared to be about fifteen. Only slightly shorter than the man, he had the same general build, lean, but wide across the shoulders. He looked more like a runner than a weight lifter.

"What a stud," Lane whispered. At fourteen, she'd become quite a connoisseur of the male sex.

"Shh," Deborah hissed.

Dr. Conover had definitely arrived. He circled the car to rest his hand on his son's shoulder and nodded toward the sign. "Looks like the town is glad to have us."

"Go to hell." The boy jerked away to stand sullenly ten feet away, his back to his father and his hands jammed deep in the pockets of his tight jeans.

Tension filled the air. Deborah reached for her nearer daughter, and Ann's fingers tightened around hers in response.

The man stared at the boy's unyielding back until the silence grew tangible, then his shoulders drooped and he gave his head a little shake. Going to the trunk, he hefted their suitcases onto the gravel. With one in each hand he walked silently to the house, ducked under the sheet and juggled keys and suitcases to unlock the door.

Both his stance and his posture alive with antagonism, the boy turned only after his father entered the house. Cursing vividly, he picked up a rock and hurled it into the bushes sheltering Deborah and the girls. Ann's grip tightened even more, and Deborah felt Lane's hand on her arm.

She'd meant the sign as a goodwill gesture. She'd hoped it would reinforce the doctor's decision to spend a year of his life in her town. Seeing his reaction, and that of his son, she wished she could snap her fingers and make it disappear.

When the boy finally grabbed his suitcases and stomped inside, her whole body seemed to unwind.

"Come on," she whispered. "Let's get out of here."

In spite of his son's attitude, the welcome sign touched Bryant. Watching it unfurl just as he entered the driveway convinced him he'd made the right decision. If, as he hoped, a different life-style could open avenues of communication, they'd come to the right place. Surely, he and Matt could mend past wounds in a town where kindhearted souls went out of their way to welcome newcomers, where mountains and clear skies formed the backdrop of life.

Inside, a cool breeze fluttered curtains at several open windows, but the house still smelled unused. Flicking on the light, he looked the place over. To his relief, he saw that it had been recently cleaned and made ready for them. Since he'd pushed the driving and arrived early, he'd expected the worst.

Matt would hate it. There was nothing elegant or expensive about this place. One big living room took up the entire front of the house, flanked on the right by a set of linoleum-covered stairs. The furniture looked comfortable. Not new, but well cared for. He ran his hand over the cast-iron surface of the wood-burning stove that filled the fireplace opening. Even if Montana winters were no worse than the ones in Milwaukee, he suspected they'd welcome it. Under the window, the boxes he'd shipped ahead waited to be unpacked.

Matt stalked into the room and dropped his bags on the floor. Sprawling on the couch, he glared at Bryant. "What a dump."

Bryant pointed to a hand-stitched yellowed sampler in a wooden frame hanging between two side windows. "No. *Home Sweet Home.*"

"Yeah, right."

Bryant understood his son's anger and feelings of betrayal, but he couldn't change past choices. He hadn't been able to undo his divorce from Nikki. He hadn't been able to stop her from keeping Matt away from him or from painting him as the villain in their breakup. Nor had he been able to keep her from abandoning Matt the year before.

On the positive side, he could be grateful she'd brought Matt to him instead of ˙dumping him on strangers. And he could save Matt from self-destruction.

By coming here, Bryant intended to have both the time and the opportunity to teach Matt some of the basic skills for living Nikki had failed to instill. He didn't expect Matt to step into a strange house in a small mountain town and be delighted with the change.

"In her last letter, Mrs. Pingree said she would prepare a bedroom for you upstairs. There's only one bathroom, though, and it's down here."

Matt muttered something under his breath which Bryant ignored. He had plenty of time to heal the wounds, nothing had to be solved tonight. So instead of arguing, he picked up his bags, turned his back on his son's hostility and started toward the back of the house.

Behind him, he heard a foot impact with a suitcase, then an exaggerated clumping up the stairs. Pausing between the living room and the hall, he leaned his shoulder heavily against the doorframe. *This would work. It had to.* He refused to consider failure. He would do anything, make any sacrifice, to build a relationship with the person he loved most in the world.

The wide, square hallway gave entrance to the kitchen on the left, the bathroom straight ahead and the bedroom to the right. Bryant went into the bedroom and flipped on the light.

Obviously never having seen the hand of an interior decorator, it welcomed him in an unassuming country-charm sort of way. A beautiful handmade quilt, pieced together in an intricate ring pattern, covered the bed. A work of art good enough to belong in a gallery, it conveyed a silent message that someone he'd never met cared what happened to him and Matt. Running his fingers over the needlework, he accepted it as a tangible affirmation. In spite of his son's anger, his father's advice and his grandfather's annoyance, he'd made the right choice in coming to Montana.

After the tools had been put away and she'd kissed the girls good-night, Deborah switched off the lights and pulled her rocking chair around so she could see the neighboring house from her living room window. Curling into the cushions, she rested her chin on her knees.

She should feel triumphant, jubilant, happy at the very least. Once again she'd managed to get a doctor for Sterling. And this time she'd insisted on a one-year contract. Signed, sealed, notarized and cast in concrete. Since establishing a small rural practice seemed to have about as much appeal as being stranded on a desert island, she'd managed to stir enough interest to get one only twice during her quest for a doctor. Both times she'd relied on a verbal agreement, and neither doctor had lasted even a month. So this time she'd gotten the commitment in writing.

Unfortunately, Dr. M. Bryant Conover III's lawyer had insisted on a two-week trial period. For two weeks, she'd be on pins and needles, hoping he didn't back out before the contract actually went into effect.

She wished she hadn't witnessed his arrival. No matter how quickly he resolved the problem with his son, she'd be replaying that scene in her mind and wondering if it had anything to do with his move to Sterling. Somehow she'd have to make the next two

weeks as positive as possible for them. Once they settled in she could relax.

At least once the doctor established his practice, she
wouldn't have to drive her mother to Bozeman once a
month. She and Glen would have a close source of
medical care for Lodestone Wilderness School. Preg-
nant women such as Brenda Wilcox wouldn't have to
deliver their babies in the back seat of a car. Men like
her father might get checkups often enough that they
wouldn't die alone on the mountain of a heart attack.
Jay would have—

No, she wouldn't think of Jay. Not now. When
Lane's fat mother cat jumped on her lap, circling and
pawing before curling into a ball, Deborah stroked her
back automatically. Next door, the living room windows went dark while a shadow moved behind the
upstairs shade. She thought of the boy's anger and
hoped he wouldn't go around slamming his fist
through walls.

Pulling her bottom lip between her teeth, she nestled deeper in the chair. Eventually, she saw the upper
bedroom light go off, leaving a single square of yellow downstairs.

Too bad Dr. Conover had arrived early, when she
had to drive her mother to Bozeman tomorrow. That
always meant staying overnight to insure Naomi didn't
get too tired. What if his son's anger stretched beyond an ordinary temper tantrum and he decided he
couldn't stay at all? What if they left before she got
back? Before she even had a chance to welcome them
properly? How ironic it would be if she lost this new
doctor while she kept an appointment with one fifty
miles away.

Since she couldn't ask her mother to postpone the appointment in Bozeman, Deborah would have to trust Dr. Conover not to give up before he started. And then she'd have to make sure he felt welcome, and help his son fit in quickly.

She'd give them a party.

It could be potluck. Since the forecast projected the weather would stay nice through the weekend, she could hold it outside. If she put the girls in charge of spreading the word and inviting the doctor, they could hold it day after tomorrow.

She saw no point in delaying. After investing years of effort and emotion into getting a doctor, she'd do anything necessary to keep him.

With Matt beside him, Bryant followed the noise to their neighbors' backyard.

The place lacked the polish common to farms in the Midwest. A hedge of unruly, almost-budding lilac divided this yard from his, and a small patch of grass filled a space between the rear of the house and an irrigation ditch. A square of half-spaded dirt looked like it would be a vegetable garden by summer, and behind it stretched a weed-infested field that might once have been productive. A dirt driveway curved toward some old, weathered sheds. And the mountains towered above everything, so close he could almost make out each individual pine.

They found the party behind the sheds.

On the bank of a pond, about thirty people milled around a fire. Some were roasting hot dogs, some were eating. Half a dozen kids gyrated to music from a boom box and stirred up the dust. Someone paddled a small canoe around the pond.

Warmth and welcome made a smile tug at the corners of Bryant's mouth. *Yes.* This was exactly the kind of environment he'd had in mind when he accepted Mrs. Pingree's invitation. Openness and community. People who lived and played together, sharing the good times, probably supporting each other during the bad ones.

Above the din, Bryant heard a shriek of laughter. He turned to see a figure in jeans swing out over the water. A heavy rope had been suspended from a tree branch at least twenty feet overhead. The length gave the pendulum a very long moment, and the water reflected the image of the person hanging on the end. On the return arc, the rope twisted and he got a good glimpse of the swinger.

It was a young woman. Her body, slim, strong and appealing, seemed part of the rope and the motion. A man on the bank gave her another push and she glided over the water again. Her auburn ponytail floated behind her head, catching the light of the late afternoon sun. Back and forth she went, higher each time as the momentum built.

"Don't fall, Debbie," someone called. "You'll get wet."

"Water's cold, Deb."

Laughter rose. Everyone at the party seemed to be watching her. Bryant understood why. Her form and movements were like music. Fluid and alive, attuned to the rhythms of nature. His eyes didn't want to be anywhere else, either.

When someone called his name, it took a second to regain his bearing.

"Dr. Conover?" A girl of about fourteen appeared at his elbow. She had flame red hair that hung in braids down her back and cheeks that dimpled engagingly. A lively sparkle in her green eyes and a mischievous grin made him wonder if she'd had some part in rigging the welcome sign over his front door.

"Yes?"

"Hi. I'm Ann. Welcome to Sterling."

"Thank you."

"We're glad you made it. We were beginning to wonder. Hey, Matt."

It took Bryant a second to realize that in two days Matt must have met quite a number of local kids.

"Hey."

Ann dimpled, and Bryant thought he detected a hint of red creep up Matt's neck. Unsure whether to be glad or wary, he decided to keep close watch on Matt with a girl this charming around.

"I was on my way to get more potato chips," Ann said. "But that can wait. Come and get something to eat."

She'd given him no information besides her first name, but her manner indicated she lived here.

"Perhaps you could introduce me to your parents first," Bryant suggested.

"I don't have a dad, but my mom wants to meet you, too. She's over there." Ann waved her hand toward the crowd at the pond. "I'll take you."

Ann led them to the group at the edge of the pond. "Mom, Dr. Conover is here."

When the people on the bank looked toward the figure on the rope, so did Bryant.

This was her mother?

Confused, he watched as the rope began to slow. Now that he had a steadier view of the woman, he could see the resemblance between her and the girl at his side. Her red hair had a darker cast to it, but her smile was just as contagious. She seemed too young to be the mother of a child this age, until he looked more closely. Then he noticed a faint network of lines at the corners of her eyes, the permanent creases that bracketed her mouth, the confidence in the way she held her head. A mixture of youth and maturity, she'd obviously met life head-on for a long time.

"Dr. Conover! I'm glad you finally made it. Did you get something to eat?" She readjusted her hold on the rope, which had slowed to sway gently over the water.

"Not yet."

"Ann, help him fill a plate."

"He wanted to meet you first."

The woman laughed, and the group joined her. "I think you have me at a disadvantage." Exaggerating her words, she looked pointedly at a man standing only a few feet from Bryant. "Thanks a lot, Glen."

It was the man who had been pushing from the bank. In his early thirties, he had a full beard and wore a cowboy hat tipped back on his head. Good-looking, seasoned, he'd looped his arm around the waist of a pretty, dark-haired woman, and a toddler clung to his leg. He raised a hand, palm up, in a gesture of helplessness. "Gee, Deb. I think you're stuck out there."

"Funny thing. I wonder how that could have happened." She shifted again, and Bryant realized she must be uncomfortable, dangling out there like that, with everyone staring at her.

He picked up a broken piece of weathered tree limb and extended it to her from the edge of the water. "Here, grab hold."

"Thanks." She linked the rope with her elbow and reached for the end of the branch. When he felt her take hold of it, he pulled her toward shore.

Laughing, she met his eyes. Hers were as vividly blue as the Montana sky. And guileless. As unlike Nikki's as eyes could be. He saw no hint of calculation or cunning, no weighing of the situation to see how she could turn it to her advantage. Instead, they spoke of a deep personal contentment, as though she hadn't a care in the world. They invited him to share her happiness. And he wanted to. With a need so deep and intense it hurt, he wanted what she had.

His hand met hers, and the spell of her eyes echoed in a spark from her fingers to his. He circled her waist and lifted her over the last half foot of water. She released the rope to rest her hands on his shoulders.

Her rich, low laughter blocked out the noise of the party. Her wildflower scent incited images of warm wind and cool nights. Her lips tempted him to sample the honey of her smile. Slowly, drinking in the new sensations she awoke in him, he lowered her to the ground.

Tiny and light, she felt fragile in his arms. Holding her, he experienced a strange feeling of recognition, as if finally meeting someone he'd been looking for for a long time.

"What a rescue!" someone exclaimed.

Bryant dropped his hands as though he'd been burned. He didn't know this woman. He didn't want to. Tomorrow he'd nod politely if he passed her on the street. He had enough on his plate without indulging an adolescent reaction to someone he'd just met.

"Thank you," she said breathlessly, smiling up at him. "My legs were starting to go to sleep."

The laughter that laced her voice made him want to smile, to touch her again, maybe to hold on and not let go. He balled his hands into fists to keep them still. "I'm sorry my arrival interrupted your swing."

"If it hadn't been you, something else would have." Glaring and smiling simultaneously at the man with a beard, she took Bryant's arm and pulled him closer. "This is Glen Halloran, a very old friend who believes it's his personal mission in life to keep me from getting complacent. His wife, Judy, and their son, Jason.

Glen grasped Bryant's hand, bringing him into the circle of their obvious friendship. "It *was* my turn, and you know it."

"So now you'd better start watching your tail." Turning back to Bryant, she offered her own hand in official greeting. "I'm Deborah Pingree."

Deborah *Pingree?* Debbie? Deb? Bryant tried to equate this petite, lively woman with his mental image of the Mrs. Pingree whose invitation had come at the right moment in his battle to save Matt. He'd guessed her to be middle-aged and managerial, rather like his mother with her social causes and civic involvement.

"Welcome to Sterling." Mrs. Pingree looped her arm around her daughter's shoulders. "You met Ann. And here's Lane." A second girl suddenly materialized at her side.

Bryant did a double take. They weren't dressed alike, and they wore their hair differently, but they were definitely identical. In his years as a family practitioner, he'd seen his share of twins, and these took the lookalike prize.

"This is my son, Matthew."

Deborah Pingree offered her hand to Matt, as easily as she had to Bryant. "I'm happy to meet you. I know Sterling won't be anything like you're used to, but it can be a nice place to live. And I'm sure we have some things to do you haven't tried before."

Matt kept his hands jammed in the pockets of his jeans.

As though she hadn't been ignored, Mrs. Pingree waved toward the fire. "Let's all go eat." And with that one quick movement, she eased the awkwardness from the situation. Bryant couldn't help admiring her style. And her hair, and the tilt of her nose...

Gritting his teeth, he tried to slam a door on the corner of his mind that kept responding to Deborah Pingree. She wasn't even that beautiful. There was just something about her that sent a rush of heat through his veins.

He couldn't let it happen again. He *had* to keep his attention focused on his son.

But she was already urging him along with a hand on his arm. "Everyone who hasn't met you yet is dying to."

Walking beside her, he noticed again how small she was. Somehow she managed to dispel the impact of her size when they talked face-to-face, but her head came barely to the top of his shoulder. Silently acknowledging the incongruity, he stopped and turned toward her. "Why didn't I know Mrs. Pingree was my next-door neighbor?"

"You didn't?" She drew her eyebrows together in thought. They were darker than her hair, with very little arch. They gave her a wholesome, unpretentious look. Abruptly, she laughed lightly. "No, I guess it hasn't come up. Well, for better or worse, we'll be liv-

ing in each other's pockets while you're here. I own the
house you're living in." Slipping her hand into his as
easily as if she'd done it all her life, she pulled him toward the picnic table near the fire. "Come on, you can
get acquainted with my mother while I find you a hot
dog."

She was a cyclone, catching him up against his will,
uprooting him and depositing him some place not of
his choosing.

The twenty yards to the picnic table took nearly half
an hour, and thankfully too many people wanted to
shake his hand for Deborah Pingree to keep hold of it.

After the first few minutes, Bryant stopped trying
to remember names. He hoped people wouldn't be
offended if he couldn't address them personally the
next time they met.

When Deborah finally presented him to her mother,
he sank onto the bench in relief.

Aside from the fact that Naomi Abbott sat in a
wheelchair, she looked like an older version of her
daughter. They had the same laughing blue eyes and
the same pert, turned-up nose, but gray had faded the
deep auburn of Naomi's hair.

Neither the mother nor the daughter commented on
the reason for the wheelchair. Bryant figured he'd find
out soon enough, since the health of the town was now
his business.

"So you're the new doctor. Sterling must be quite a
change from Milwaukee." Welcome and enthusiasm
colored Naomi's voice, just as it did her daughter's.

"My specialty is family medicine. I thought it would
be beneficial to gain some experience in a small town."
A true if incomplete answer. As his grandfather had
been quick to point out, Bryant's future didn't re-

quire this kind of additional preparation. On the other hand, it wouldn't hurt.

"Oh, I'm sure it is," Naomi agreed. "And you couldn't have picked a nicer place than Sterling. How does your son like it?"

Automatically, Bryant turned to check. But Matt stood to one side, apart and alone. "He seems to be having a hard time fitting in. Maybe I should go talk to him."

Before he could leave the bench, one of the twins approached Matt, with a hot dog speared on a stick in one hand and a paper cup in the other.

Mrs. Abbott nodded with obvious pride. "That's Lane. She should be able to make him feel right at home. There's nothing bashful about either of those girls."

"You must be very proud of them."

"Here." Deborah appeared suddenly and thrust a stick at him. He took it as tentatively as Matt had accepted the one from Lane. "This is a cook-your-own kind of party. Mom will excuse us. You can come back and flirt with her later."

Only one person at the party tempted Bryant to flirt, and he'd already decided to keep himself immune to her.

She led him to the fire, then went off to see to other guests. Almost immediately one of the twins brought him a bun and chattered to him while he stuck the meat into the flame and tried to keep it from burning. Since the girl Naomi Abbott called Lane was still with Matt, Bryant assumed this was Ann.

Listening to the daughter, his eyes followed the mother. Irresistibly. And in watching her, he learned a great deal about the kind of woman she was.

She managed to be everywhere, mingling constantly, keeping people involved, offering more food, refilling cups. Bryant saw her coax one of the older men down to the pond and insist he ride the rope. Gamely, her victim hooked his foot into the loop, laughing as she pushed him off.

"That's the way, Sam. Hold on."

A woman, obviously Sam's wife, watched from the bank a little uneasily. But Sam held firm while Deborah pushed, and when he finished, he leapt nimbly to the ground.

"Now tell me that's not still fun," Deborah prodded.

"Oh, it's fun. But, I swear, one of these days you'll be the death of me, girl."

It occurred to Bryant that Deborah Pingree might be as much like his mother as he'd first assumed. This party was as remote from the formal affairs Caroline Conover presided over as Sterling was from Milwaukee, but Caroline would never allow the pace of one of her parties to drag, either. She, too, always made sure everyone felt included. And like his mother, Deborah seemed to do it without giving her guests the slightest hint they were being handled by a master.

And there was something about her that kept her from dissolving into this crowd of new faces. Her movements were quick and purposeful, yet smooth and satisfying to watch. While he'd never been particularly attracted to small women, Deborah seemed alive with an inner fire, a fire that people automatically responded to. God knew, he responded to it.

He glanced down at the girl beside him.

"People in this town love your mother, don't they?"

Her expression told him it went without saying. "Of course. She's wonderful."

He grinned and thought of the welcome sign. "In spite of having you two."

"Oh, we're wonderful, too," she replied without missing a beat.

"So, how do people tell you and your sister apart?"

"They can't. Except for Mom. And she taught us that it wasn't fair to switch, so we only do it when we absolutely have to."

"Like for tests?" he inquired artlessly.

She just smiled and looked mysterious.

"How old are you?"

"Fourteen."

"Ninth grade?"

"Only for one more month."

"Are all the boys in love with you?"

She wrinkled her nose and shook her head. "We have red hair."

"So does your mother."

"But she's beautiful!"

Bryant's eyes found Deborah Pingree again. "Yes, she is."

Chapter Two

Deborah caught herself watching the doctor and jerked her eyes away. What a fool she'd made of herself! Drooling over him in front of thirty of her closest friends—none of whom would hesitate to give an opinion or offer advice. Or encouragement. And things would only get worse if she kept staring at him.

But how could she help it? She hadn't met a man in thirteen years who made her pulse race.

He was shorter than he'd seemed when she'd been in the bushes looking up, perhaps about five-ten. His hair was dark blond, his eyes dark hazel, and he smiled rarely. But when he'd put his hands on her waist to lift her off the rope, something bright and buoyant had opened inside her. The smile she'd seen then, in his eyes and teasing at the corners of his mouth, had made her headier than swinging on the rope.

A rush like that might be good for the female ego, especially one as rusted as hers. But like an eddy in a stream, it didn't affect the steady flow of life. She would concentrate on making Dr. Conover's first two weeks in Sterling as stress free as possible, then the current would catch her back up again.

She let him finish eating before collecting him from Ann to introduce him to the people he hadn't met. He greeted them with none of the condescension one of her previous doctors had radiated. He paid attention when they spoke to him. Even Ivy Hilgendorff, who held him captive with a flow of questions about her degenerating health.

When someone turned the tape over on the boom box, Deborah decided to rescue him from Ivy.

"Come dance. You'll never see a floor like this in your big city." His loafers and the hems of his slacks were already gray with dust, but if he minded he didn't let it show.

"I didn't expect it to be the same here. I hoped it wouldn't be."

"Then I'm happy to meet your expectations in one small way. You'll probably get sick of hearing me say this, but I'm glad you decided to come. It means a lot to me."

"Your invitation arrived at an opportune time. Matt and I both needed a change." Even as he started moving to the beat of the music, his eyes searched for Matt.

Trying to fit what she'd seen this afternoon with the scene she'd witnessed on their arrival, she wondered what the problem was. Every time Dr. Conover looked at his son or said his name, he tightened up. If making it through his trial period depended on his relationship with Matt, what could she say or do to tip the balance?

If only Matt could get used to living here. A few minutes earlier, Lane had prodded him back to the fire to roast marshmallows. They were still at it, but Matt didn't look as if he were having the best time of his life.

Suddenly his marshmallow caught fire. He jerked it from the flame, and Lane grabbed the stick to keep burning sugar from flying into someone's hair or face.

Matt must have misunderstood. Practically throwing his end of the stick at her, he stomped away. Poor Lane watched in stunned silence, and Deborah saw the uncertainty in her daughter's face. Should she follow him and try to make it all right?

Bryant didn't share Lane's indecision. He immediately started after his son.

Deborah checked him instinctively with a hand on his arm. "Let him go." She might not know the source of Matt's problems, but she understood teenagers.

"I beg your pardon?" A moment ago, the doctor had been easing toward another smile. Now he looked down at her with stone-cold eyes.

She shifted uncomfortably. It was none of her business, but she'd already stuck her foot in it. "Would he welcome anything you could do?"

"What would you know about it?"

She heard the scorn, and the hurt. But he was right, she didn't know either of them at all. She only knew what she'd seen. "He was looking for a reason to leave."

"And he found it. Now, if you'll excuse me."

Stunned and embarrassed, Deborah watched Bryant Conover follow his son toward the house next door. It was over. Just because she'd let her impulses guide her. Between Matt's attitude and her own interference, the new doctor could easily decide this wasn't going to work and be on his way back to Milwaukee by morning.

And because she'd agreed to a stupid trial period, he'd get away with it. And Sterling would once again be without any health care at all.

By the time Bryant reached the house, Matt had his music on full blast. The pounding bass reverberated through the floor, as unrelenting as a migraine, as aggressive as an enemy.

Driven by a potent mix of anger, embarrassment and concern, he started up the stairs two at a time.

Before he got halfway, reason reasserted itself and he slumped against the wall.

What would he gain by storming into Matt's room like Sherman marching to the sea? Nothing. Relieved he'd managed not to make things worse by losing his temper, he turned back down the stairs.

At the party, he'd begun to hope they'd turned some invisible corner. In the ten months Matt had lived with Bryant, he'd shown little interest in making friends— but he seemed to get along with the kids here. Then the smallest thing had triggered a tantrum, and Bryant knew they hadn't budged from dead center. Not if a cute, personable girl such as Lane Pingree couldn't bring Matt out of his isolation.

But he hadn't decided to come here on the off chance Matt would find nice friends. Passing through the living room to the kitchen, he went to the back window and looked out at the mountains.

Since Deborah Pingree's first letter, he'd been imagining how those mountains could help him salvage his relationship with Matt. They offered rugged togetherness. Camping, fishing, hiking. Male bonding. In learning new skills at the same time, he and Matt would have to rely on each other.

The mountains called to him. In his mind's eye Bryant saw tall stands of pine, swift-running rivers, a trout leaping for a fly, a tent pitched under the stars. He ached to sit across a campfire from Matt in newfound camaraderie. Though it might be nothing but fantasy, it pumped through his veins like a promise, and he wanted it to start today. This minute.

Taking the stairs two at a time, Bryant knocked on Matt's door and went in. Matt lay on the bed, his hands linked behind his head and his eyes focused on the ceiling.

Taking first things first, Bryant switched off the stereo.

"Get lost," Matt said, his voice flat and cold.

"I want to talk to you about this weekend."

Silence.

"I thought we could go camping."

Matt's upper lip curled into a sneer. "Like you know anything about that stuff."

"We can learn."

"Yeah, right."

"I could pick you up from school on Friday and we could spend a couple of nights."

More silence.

"We're here. Let's take advantage of it. You might find—"

In one swift, jerky movement, Matt rolled off the bed and swung on Bryant. "Look, I'm not your *buddy*, okay? You don't give a damn about me. You never have. I hate this place and I hate you."

In the space of a second, hurt bloomed and burst into anger. Bryant caught Matt's arm with one hand and captured his jaw with the other. He held his son's face until their eyes met. Fear flashed in Matt's, then sharpened into scorn. Suddenly Bryant realized how close they'd both come to a physical confrontation. How close he'd come to taking his nearly grown son across his knee.

Force wasn't his way. In his practice at Conover Memorial he'd seen too many examples of child abuse to let himself skirt the edges of it. "I'm sorry," he said.

"Go to hell."

His arms ached to take Matt into them. They'd lost thirteen years because Nikki had wanted to hurt Bryant by keeping his son from him. Ten months ago she'd remarried and given Matt back at the insistence of her new husband, but by then the damage had been done. Time gaped between them like an abyss, and Bryant didn't know how to cross it. He couldn't remember ever getting more than a handshake from his own father, and although many times that had been enough, it gave him no help in dealing with Matt. Especially since Matt rejected all his attempts to discuss the past in the reasoned, logical Conover manner Bryant's father had always used with him.

"Keep the volume on your stereo down for the rest of the evening." Not waiting for an answer, Bryant turned and went downstairs. His heart hammered against his ribs and the back of his neck was clammy with sweat. The months ahead looked long and rocky, and not for the first time fear that things would never get better twisted inside him.

No! He refused to accept that. He'd been given a second chance and a new opportunity. He opened the refrigerator and checked the contents. Milk, soda, O.J. Nothing stronger, nothing to drown his apprehensions. He pulled a Mountain Dew from its harness.

In the absence of Matt's stereo, he could hear Deborah Pingree's party still going full swing. He'd probably made a wonderful impression, leaving so abruptly.

On the other hand, why should she take offense? She was the one who had stuck her nose in where it didn't belong. Where did she get off, telling him how to respond to his son? How could she imagine she understood the situation with Matt? No one else did.

Just thinking about it, an unfamiliar resentment tugged at him. She had everything. Dozens of friends. A supportive mother. Two sweetheart daughters, who probably never gave her a moment's concern.

Perhaps she was also in the habit of minding everyone else's business. If so, this evening's little episode was a warning. He should keep a safe distance from her. Of course that might be difficult, since she was both his sponsor in this town and his landlady.

He leaned his shoulder against the window frame and listened. A wave of laughter from the party rolled up from the pond. In his mind's eye, he saw her. Laughing, dancing, reaching out her hand to someone. He saw the honesty in her blue eyes, felt the acceptance in her touch, remembered how holding her had made the rest of the world fade into a blur. A sudden heat flooded through his veins and tightened into a knot in his chest.

Since his divorce from Nikki, he'd applied himself strictly to his career, keeping his friendships with women cool and platonic. What did they say? Once burned, twice shy? He still bore the scars from the burn Nikki had inflicted.

But something about Deborah Pingree opened a window into his soul, spilling long-buried needs into the open. Needs for feminine companionship, for gentleness and joy. With difficulty, he pulled himself away from the window and shuttered the view in his mind.

He couldn't think about her. Wouldn't. Matt meant more to him than life itself. He'd seen tonight how tenuous each step with Matt would be. He needed to keep all his energy focused on breaking down the walls.

Letting anything distract him could cost him what he valued most. His son.

Deborah hid from curious friends and neighbors by attacking the shelves of jeans located at the rear of the store. The gossipmongers had started arriving within minutes of opening, eager to rehash the party—and confirm an unbelievable variety of speculations.

Today the mess of jeans wasn't as bad as in the fall when kids shopped for school clothes, but the sizes were mixed and the 505s were jumbled up with the 501s. The trouble was, sorting stonewashed from blues from grays didn't take much concentration.

The party had been a total bomb. Oh, the locals had had a good time, but the guests of honor hadn't exactly wiped their feet on the welcome mat. All her efforts to find a doctor for Sterling were probably down the drain again, and this time she had no one to blame but herself. But even if she'd kept her impulses to herself, there was no guarantee Dr. Conover would last the trial period. Not as much as his son seemed to hate it here.

Was there anything she could do to redeem the situation?

Take a plate of cookies and apologize? Beg on her hands and knees? Line up a hundred patients to show him how much the town needed him? How much she needed him as a doctor?

For thirteen years, bringing medical care to Sterling had topped her priority list. That Dr. Conover happened to be particularly attractive didn't change a thing. She wanted him for his skill, his education, his experience. Not for the way his gray green eyes exactly matched the leaves of a Russian olive tree in summer. Or for the appeal of a slightly crooked left eyetooth. Or because the little tuft of chest hair that curled in the open placket of his polo shirt invited her fingers to touch him right there.

She wanted to know that someone unlocked old Doc Bennion's office every morning. She wanted the reassurance that if one of the twins broke an arm in the dead of winter, she could get it fixed without driving fifty miles on treacherous mountain roads.

When Judy Halloran materialized suddenly and propped her hip against the shelves, Deborah decided it was a gift from heaven. Sorting jeans had done nothing to divert her thoughts.

"What are you doing hiding back here?" Judy demanded.

"Hiding."

"Well, it didn't work. My word, you and the doctor sure had sparks flying last night. You nearly lit up the sky."

Or maybe a curse from hell. "I don't know what you're talking about."

Judy only laughed. "I say go for it. A guy that good-looking moves in next door, you'd be a fool to let the opportunity pass you by."

Deliberately, Deborah slid the stack of jeans into its place on the shelf. Hoping she had control of her emotions, and therefore her expression, she looked Judy straight in the eye. "I hope you're not suggesting I have an affair with him."

"Why not? The attraction seemed to be mutual. You're both unattached and reasonably good-looking."

"So without further consideration of the consequences, Deb Pingree walks to the edge of the cliff and jumps off."

Judy dropped to her knees and laid her hand over Deborah's. "Or you could go the rest of your life without a little romance."

With a light laugh, she turned her fingers over to squeeze Judy's. "I happen to like my life just fine, thank you very much."

"It's been a long time since Jay—"

"Jay would want me to be happy, and I am. I'm also too busy for complications."

With a sigh, Judy stood up and reached a hand down to Deborah. "I hope that doesn't mean you can't slip away for a cherry Coke. Jason's grandma's got him this morning, and I need someone to share my freedom. See if Charlie can watch the store."

Deborah scanned the half-straightened shelves of jeans. "I might as well. These will be back to normal by noon."

"All the more reason not to bother."

After telling her assistant manager she'd be at the drugstore a while, Deborah followed Judy out into the bright spring sunlight.

While waiting for his next patient, Bryant looked out his office window at Sterling's main street. A pickup drove by, dusty and dented, with a gun rack in the rear window. It looked like it spent a lot of time on unpaved mountain roads. Its driver probably knew every trout stream between here and Bozeman.

With a wry smile, Bryant considered what he knew about fishing. One used either flies or bait. One stood on the bank or waded into the water. Fish had to be cleaned once they were caught. That was it. If he expected Matt to experience the pleasure of winning against a trophy cutthroat, they probably ought to find a good teacher to start with. He'd have to ask Deborah Pingree where to find one.

Deborah Pingree, the woman who had opened the door of opportunity for him. The woman who kept stealing little pieces of his mind by filling it with questions about her.

Questions like why had she gone to so much effort to bring a doctor to Sterling? So far he'd seen a dozen patients, but they'd all been more curious than ill.

Why had looking into her eyes made him feel like a kid again, ripe for adventure and hungry for intimacy?

Why did a woman like her live in a town like Sterling? Even if she'd grown up here, why did she stay?

Why did he keep thinking of her? He had a job to do and a son to save, and nothing else mattered. Period. He wondered when he'd stop having to remind himself.

Following old habits, he went automatically to the examining room. It was empty. The waiting room was empty. Curious, he checked the appointment book and found he had half an hour before his next appointment.

Since he'd never before had an idle minute during the middle of the day, he decided to make the most of it. He would walk down the hill on one side of the street and come back up the other to get a closer look at downtown Sterling. Then he'd stop in at the general store again and see if he could find someone to introduce him to the fine art of casting a line.

As he neared the drugstore, he saw Deborah Pingree come out with Judy Halloran. They were laughing, as though neither of them had a worry in the world. Or at least, as if they had all the answers and none of them hurt.

Next to Deborah, Judy seemed taller than he'd remembered from the party, but just as pretty. Although her clothes were standard Sterling, with her dark good looks she might have stepped straight from the pages of a fashion magazine,

Yet it was Deborah who made him look twice. Her jeans molded her slender hips and her T-shirt hugged her breasts. Her face seemed to radiate an inner fire, like some mystical quality that could grab a man in the gut and not let go.

The images he'd spent the night fighting flowed back through his mind. The fluid movement of her body swinging over the water, her weight in his arms, the jerk of his pulse when she met his eyes.

Today, her hair was loose, held back on the sides with matching clips. It flowed around her shoulders in an aureole of sunlight, as if she took her energy from the sky. Even from a distance she pulled at him, like a force too strong to resist.

"Dr. Conover!" Seeing him, her laughter stopped. The hesitation lasted only a moment, then she smiled and heat rolled across his skin. "How are things going? Is your office working out all right? Has everyone in town been in for you to look down their throats? Do you still need anything? Are you in a hurry to get back?"

Her questions came too fast, as if driven by uncertainty, but they pulled him back to reality and reminded him he had a hundred reasons to be pleasant—and nothing more.

"I have another appointment in a few minutes."

Skillfully, she began to create a conversation that included both him and Judy. If he weren't careful, she'd pull him into the current of this town whether he liked it or not.

To his surprise, Judy glanced abruptly at her watch. "I'm afraid I've got to run. I promised Glen's mom I'd pick Jason up by eleven. It was good to see you again, Bryant. I'll call you, Deb." With a wave, she hurried across the street to her car.

Bryant turned to Deborah. The wildflower scent of her hair made him want to run his fingers through it. "Where are you headed?" he asked politely.

"To the Merc. I slipped away in the middle of the day, too. Maybe it's the weather, do you think? Too nice to stay cooped up inside?" In spite of himself, he allowed her to lead him across the street. As they walked she kept her face tilted toward his.

"The Merc?" Matching her shorter stride, Bryant tried not to remember how perfectly she had fit against him when he'd helped her off the rope. It was a sensation he couldn't afford to indulge.

"Sterling Mercantile." With a light laugh, she waved her hand in an all-encompassing gesture. "The place where you buy groceries, hardware, dry goods and fertilizer. Unless you want to drive to Bozeman for better prices and a better selection."

He nodded. This seemed a safe enough topic. "I was just headed there. It's a fascinating place."

"You think so?"

It was his turn to laugh. "That store carries the broadest variety of products I've ever seen. I could spend hours browsing around."

"You could?" He heard both disbelief and satisfaction in her voice.

"Is that so surprising?"

"Well, it's always seemed sort of dingy to me. I keep thinking I'm going to replace the floor coverings, or at least the lights, but then I end up spending my profits somewhere else."

"You own it?"

Her eyebrows arched and she nodded. "I guess there are a lot of things I ought to tell you about this town." They reached the store, but Deborah didn't go in. Instead, she leaned her back against the wall and turned her face into the sun. "That is, if you want me to." This time the tiniest hint of hope, or need, curled around her words.

"Of course. Sterling's not what I expected, but then I'm not sure what I thought I'd find. It's interesting." *You're interesting.* He caught himself from saying it out loud, tried to resist thinking it at all.

"I guess it must seem a little provincial to you."

How could a town of less than five hundred people be anything but very provincial? Bryant chose a neutral answer. "Colorful. Cordial."

Her laugh rang out again, sparkling and unaffected. "I like that. Maybe I'll propose that the town council put up a new welcome sign. Something big and flashy that says WELCOME TO STERLING, CORDIAL AND COLORFUL GATEWAY TO THE HIGH COUNTRY."

"You could make it white, with fluorescent green lettering."

She ducked her head, and for the first time since they'd met she seemed to have nothing to say.

"I liked the sign." He watched in fascination as embarrassment changed to hesitation. She pulled her bottom lip between her teeth, then drew a slow, deep breath before lifting her face again. Seeing her like this, unsure and awkward, made him feel strangely protective.

"I wasn't sure you did."

"It was a nice gesture."

She began to relax again, slowly, and the smile crept back into her eyes. Lifting one shoulder, as though still uncertain, she grinned. "Ever since you arrived I've been wishing we hadn't done it."

"Why?"

But she only shook her head. "It's not every day we get a doctor."

"That's something I've been wanting to ask you about. Why *did* you want a doctor? So far I haven't seen much need."

A shadow flicked in her eyes. "People get sick in Sterling, just like everywhere else. They have accidents."

He knew she was holding back. This sounded personal, and deep. Her mother perhaps. As soon as he returned to the office he'd ask his nurse about Naomi Abbott. "But you're the one who requested a doctor. Why? Or were you just the emissary?"

"Oh, I claim full responsibility for bringing you here." When she lifted her head, determination filled her expression. "This area has been without a permanent doctor for more than fifteen years. Twice before you, I managed to convince doctors to come. Neither of them lasted."

Perhaps this was the source of the plea he'd heard in her voice. "I'm going to stay. We agreed on a year, and I'm probably going to need the full time."

Suddenly, Deborah touched his arm. "How was Matt this morning? Did he get over whatever was bothering him last night?"

Her questions brought him up firmly against reality. Last night she'd overstepped the bounds, and she was on the verge of doing it again. He didn't need her sympathy, and he didn't need her interference.

"It's something we have to work out in private."

She looked up in surprise. "I just thought if there was anything I could do..."

He'd been too sharp; he saw it in her face. But Matt was his problem, and his alone. "I don't think so."

"I mean, I do know this town—"

She did, and he needed help learning about both it and the area. But if he turned to her for help, who would help him stay focused on Matt? "I'll let you know." Glancing at his watch, he saw to his dismay that he'd spent nearly half an hour with her. Thirty minutes that had been too pleasant. So pleasant he'd neglected his responsibilities. Patients would again be filling the waiting room. "I think I'd better get back."

"I'm sure of it. Or Shirley will have your head."

The wry note in her voice surprised him; it shaved the edge off his temper. From what he'd seen so far of the woman who'd renewed a nursing license to help him, Deborah was right. He smiled reluctantly, anticipating the lecture he'd get on his return. "I thought it was my imagination."

Deborah's eyes widened and she shook her head. "Hardly."

"Then I'm already in trouble."

Before he could turn away, her hand touched his arm. As if zapped by a current, his heart jerked in his chest at the contact. It felt too good to pull away.

"I thought you'd be gone this morning," she said. "After last night, I didn't think there was any way you'd stay. I didn't mean to butt in where I wasn't wanted. I promised myself that if you were still here today I wouldn't do it again. I'm sorry."

Meeting her eyes, listening to the honesty in her voice, Bryant reluctantly admitted that this woman roused feelings he'd been trying to kill with willpower and logic. A fierce, unbidden desire coursed through his veins.

He reined it quickly under control.

Who was Deborah Pingree? The person who provided the chance he'd need with Matt. A genius with words and sympathy. A woman able to ignite long-dead coals of desire. He knew he couldn't let it mean anything, but standing there, in the middle of town, in the broad light of day, he wanted to kiss her.

Abruptly, he pivoted away toward his office. He couldn't remember ever being barraged by such a plethora of confusing emotions. But he knew himself well, and he knew he could control them.

Well, so much for thinking a break would take her mind off Bryant Conover. Just meeting his eyes made her heart pound. Hearing his rare, low-pitched laughter sent goose bumps racing down her spine.

Deborah pressed her palms against the warm brick behind her and closed her eyes. She'd never expected to feel such things again, she'd never wanted to. Now the impact of her reaction to Bryant Conover frightened her. She knew it had nothing to do with love. Love grew slowly and took steady nurturing. Love required commitment and trust. But even giving it some casual name like physical attraction, it still felt like betrayal.

Oh, Jay. There will never be anyone else for me.

Obviously, she had two choices. Ignore Dr. Conover altogether, or convince herself he was just another male friend, like Glen or Charlie or Sam O'Roark. In a town the size of Sterling she could hardly ignore him, especially when she'd personally invited him to town and he lived next door.

Forcing herself, Deborah watched Bryant stride down the street and consciously layered indifference over every word, every touch, every exchange of eye contact. She pictured herself running into him again and greeting him the way she would if she'd known him all her life. After a dozen or so tries, she managed to make it work. In her mind. And that was half the battle. Wasn't it?

Chapter Three

As though the words would be different the second time through, Deborah started to reread the letter from a supplier she'd relied on for years. When she got to "We are unable to extend . . ." she wadded up the paper and hurled it into the corner of her small office. Dammit. Didn't her track record mean anything at all?

"I have a very good bedside manner, if you'd care to talk about it."

She spun her old oak office chair around to find Bryant Conover at the door. Of all the people to witness her show of temper, why did it have to be him? Chagrined, she smiled up at him.

"I doubt a prescription would solve my problem."

"So the symptoms aren't physical?"

"Not physiological, at any rate."

"Mental?"

"Only as in anguish."

It took him two strides to cross the small floor of her office, which wasn't enough time for her to realize his purpose and prepare herself. He cupped her chin with his hand and tilted it to look into her eyes. In his office, his touch might have seemed as distant and professional as that of any doctor. In hers, it felt personal. And intimate. Heat spread from his fingers to her throat to her spine.

"Should I administer first aid?"

"For what? A wounded ego?"

"Or a loss of good spirits?"

"Do you give humor transfusions?"

"Only if the recipient's in dire straights. Are you?"

"Am I what?" *Giddy, and getting worse? Losing my grip on reality? Succumbing to your charm? All of the above?*

Suddenly, he dropped his hand and stepped away. His eyes darkened in an abrupt change of mood. "No. Anguish is just a word to you, isn't it?"

She struggled for control. One second his expression had been warm and inviting. The next, a glacial chill frosted his words. She didn't know what had changed, but whatever had passed between them in those few seconds of physical contact might never have existed. Once again he'd become the troubled man with a troubled son. And trying to empathize by recounting her own history of personal woe wouldn't help.

She grabbed the first neutral subject to cross her mind, and hoped for the best. "A word that's probably a little strong for this situation. A supplier just turned down my application for a line of credit, even though I've been buying from them for years. But I'm sure that's not what you came to see me about."

"Actually, I came looking for Matt. He was supposed to spend the morning doing homework, but no one answered the phone when I called to check on him. Shirley thought you might know where he is."

Deborah laughed. It came out a little ragged, laced with the shreds of Bryant's emotional pull, but it helped steady her. "The village grapevine at work. He came here looking for a job."

"And you gave him one?"

"Shouldn't I have?"

"He's had too much money all his life."

Maybe if he'd never touched her. Maybe if she hadn't reacted like a schoolgirl. And maybe if he hadn't pulled back so completely, so fast, she would have dealt with him differently now. But his attitude merely fueled her temper. He teased her emotions, and he seemed to have little empathy for his son. She couldn't rationalize her own response, but she could defend Matt.

"How much of it did he have to earn himself?"

Bryant's narrowed eyes bored into hers. She refused to look away.

To her relief, before the apology forming in her mind could break free, he shrugged and backed away. "I guess there aren't that many places to spend it around here."

"The temptations are out there. That doesn't mean a job's a bad idea."

A humorless smile touched his lips. "I guess it depends on whether it keeps a kid out of trouble or if it enables him to indulge, doesn't it?"

"Yes, I guess it does. I'll take you to him."

Bryant stayed close as Deborah wound her way through the store. Too close. In the wide aisles, their shoulders brushed; in the narrow ones, she could feel his presence inches from her back. He might have mentally brushed aside that brief tête-à-tête, but the impression of his fingers remained on her chin.

So much for thinking that through pure strength of will she could stop reacting to him like a hormone-driven teenager. She quickened her pace to get a step or two ahead of him, then kept the distance all the way to the heavy swinging doors that separated the main part of the store from the warehouse section.

The minute she stepped through them, he moved close beside her again. She meant to take him straight to Matt, but he stopped her with a hand on her arm.

"What is all this?"

Deborah tried to see the activity through a newcomer's eyes. Without knowing what the various piles of equipment were for, it would look bewildering.

"Lodestone Wilderness School. We take twelve to fifteen people at a time up into the mountains and teach them outdoor and survival skills. The group leaving tomorrow is all beginners, so we send up enough food for the week. They'll learn to set up a camp, build fires, cook, read maps, load a pack horse, that sort of thing."

Silently insisting she didn't care what he thought, Deborah watched Bryant's face as he took it all in. Confusion came first, then awareness, and finally interest. "Is this a service your store provides?"

She shook her head. "The school's separate from the store. When I was growing up, my dad operated a guide service, mostly for hunters. He started taking me and my brother and sister when we were younger than the twins, and then Glen and Jay began to come along, too. It was Dad who suggested we teach classes, and the school grew from there. We incorporated it five years ago.''

"I haven't met Jay, have I?" Bryant asked.

"He was my husband," she said without emphasis. "He died when the girls were babies."

"I'm sorry." Sudden mortification filled his voice, as if he'd just committed a major social blunder.

So, it was his turn to take a wrong step from lack of information. Deborah quelled a sense of satisfaction. "It happened a long time ago. Do you want to say hello to Matt?''

"I doubt he'd welcome me."

Deborah considered the kids at work. Ann sat on an upended crate with a clipboard on her lap. As she read from a list, Lane and Matt counted off items before passing them on to Glen, who packed them into the truck. How would it feel to be so insecure about a relationship with your own child that you had to evaluate whether or not to say hello?

"Come on. It won't be so bad."

But as they started toward the kids, Bryant's tension become more palpable with each step. For his sake, Deborah wanted to take his hand and offer moral support. For Matt's she wanted to tell him to loosen up, to expect the best instead of the worst and see what happened. For her own, she kept her hands and her opinion to herself.

"Not They Might Be Giants," they heard Ann say. "They're too ridiculous."

"REM," Lane said.

"No." Ann shook her head decisively. "They're too esoteric."

"That's what I like about them."

"Midnight Oil," Matt said. "They sing about issues, important things."

"Cool," Lane agreed.

Still halfway across the room, Bryant slowed his pace. "Issues? I thought he only liked loud."

"Do you know anything about rock music?" Deborah asked.

"Not a thing."

"Neither do I." While she often enjoyed the beat of her daughters' music, she'd never listened closely enough to differentiate the groups or learn many lyrics. Give her George Strait or Wynonna Judd any day. "I especially wouldn't know that Midnight Oil is issue minded."

"Or that REM is esoteric," Bryant agreed. "Do you think she knows what that means?"

"Probably. Ann takes debate. It gives her a lot broader vocabulary than I had at that age."

"Hey, Mom!" Seeing them, Lane skipped across the floor and grabbed Deborah's hand.

"We want to take Matt up to Hidden Lake for a cookout. Say yes—please, please, please."

Over her daughter's head, Deborah met Bryant's eyes, but she found no answering amusement there. Which shouldn't be surprising. Given Matt's temperament, he'd probably never experienced a teenager's urgent pleading. She realized it was a blessing she hadn't fully appreciated.

"Hidden Lake? In April?"

"Oh, yeah. It'll still be snowed in. How about Moose Flats?"

"That sounds a little better for this time of year."

"How about tomorrow?"

"After church."

Lane pivoted for a silent consultation with her twin, which brought Ann into the circle. Joined forces. It was a good thing Deborah had long ago learned how to avoid being overpowered. Matt followed Ann, but stayed in the background.

"Can we invite a few more kids, so Matt can get to know people?" Ann asked.

"Jessica and who else?" Deborah asked, hazarding a guess that the twins' best friend would be first on the list.

"Scott and Nathan."

"And Mary Margaret," Lane concluded.

"I think we could manage that."

Suddenly, Lane turned to Bryant. "You can come, too, if you want."

Bryant's eyes immediately sought Matt's. Deborah saw Matt's expression darken, then turn blank. Never looking at his father, he turned his shoulder to the group. An ache tugged at her heart for both of them and whatever had brought them to this point.

"I don't think—"

"Oh, come on. You'll love Moose Flats."

"I'm sure I would, but—"

"Leave the doctor alone, Lane. If he doesn't want to come, he has every right to say no."

"But I'm sure you don't want to be the only adult."

"I've managed before."

Lane lowered her voice almost to a whisper. "But what if Matt won't come unless his dad does?"

Before Deborah could point out that Matt might come only if Bryant *didn't,* Ann grabbed Matt's arm. "Tell him to come. He'll listen to you."

With a hard little smile, Matt cast a black, challenging look at Bryant. "Yeah. Come."

Tension rolled between them like charged thunder ready to strike. If Matt imagined Bryant would back down, he'd underestimated his father. A muscle twitched in Bryant's jaw before he dropped his eyes to Lane. "Thank you for inviting me. Of course I'll come."

The heat of anger blazed in Matt's face, then he swung around and headed back to the truck to help Glen.

Deborah drew a deep breath to ease her dread. She expected Sunday afternoon to be anything but a picnic. But when her eyes connected with Bryant's over the heads of the twins, something fast and fleeting passed between them, and she suspected fireworks between Bryant and Matt were the least of her worries.

Suddenly impatient with herself, she stiffened her spine. If seven teenagers couldn't provide enough confusion to maintain a reasonable distance between herself and Bryant, nothing could.

Bryant had wanted a teacher. He'd imagined a grizzled, middle-aged mountain man with a weather eye and animal instincts. How could he have guessed the foremost local expert would be the first woman to set his senses on edge in fifteen years?

Deborah Pingree tempted him. Her translucent skin invited him to smooth his fingers across it. He flattened his palms on his thighs to keep from stretching his arm along the back of the seat and resting his hand against her cheek.

Today her hair was french braided down the back of her head and tied with a green ribbon on the end. What little makeup she wore didn't cover a sprinkling of freckles on her nose and cheeks. Her blue eyes smiled often, and she kept taking one hand or the other off the steering wheel to identify various landmarks for him.

She talked about the mountains that provided a backdrop for the town as though they were alive. They had names and moods and personalities. Some were harsher than others, some more difficult to know.

He struggled to make casual conversation. "You said your father was a guide?"

"And an outfitter. I don't know when he started. It was just something he always did. Even when I was a kid, people would want him to lead them into the mountains. Mostly men, and usually to hunt. Backpacking got really popular in the late sixties, and that's when he started taking us with him."

"You must have been a baby."

She shot him a look full of laughter. "I was eight." Leaning over the steering wheel, she pointed high to the left. "Six years ago, he had a group of four hunters with him at nearly nine thousand feet when he died of a heart attack. There was nothing they could do but bring him back." A deep, warm chuckle spilled free and she shook her head. "I missed him like crazy for a long, long time, but bless his heart, he always said he would die doing what he liked best."

Bryant had a sudden memory of his grandfather, standing in front of the fireplace in his dark, tall-ceilinged library, lifting his glass to toast the new year. "Here's to living the life you wanted, and to doing what you love until the end." That had been four years ago, and now he was eighty-three—still strong and aggressive, still living the life he wanted. And he would die doing what he loved. No wonder Deborah remembered her father with such affection.

The road changed from asphalt to dirt, abruptly becoming rougher. When they took a particularly steep incline, a girl in the back squealed. A camper shell kept the kids secure, but there were no seats. They'd all just crawled into the back, and Bryant could imagine them sliding into each other with each bump and curve. He heard the rumble of male laughter and hoped Matt was enjoying himself.

"The kids love this place, " Deborah said. "Almost as much as Hidden Lake."

Bryant could see why. Rugged and wild, new yellow greens joined the darker shadows of the pines, patches of snow still hugged the north slopes. And following the curve of the mountain, the road often provided a view of the valley below.

"How much farther?" he asked.

"Just another mile or so. Tired of the ride?"

"It's rough."

As if to illustrate the point, another squeal rose from the back. The truck climbed suddenly as the road crested a ridge, forcing Bryant deeper into the seat. Coincidentally, more laughter from the back of the truck surged through the cab. When they leveled, Deborah turned off the road, bumping into a small meadow.

"Here we are. Moose Flats."

Straight ahead, the mountain climbed steeply, raw and primitive. To their left a stream separated the clearing from brush and forest. Behind them and to the right, the road followed the curve of the meadow before disappearing into more woods.

"Why is it called Moose Flats?" Bryant asked.

"Who knows? Because some old geezer saw a moose here once, probably." She twisted in her seat and tapped the window, but the kids had already piled out.

One of the twins began issuing instructions. "We have to have a fire first, and it's going to take a lot of wood."

Bryant decided it must be Ann. She seemed the more managerial of the two. Within seconds, all the kids were off on their errands. Deborah hooked her hands in her rear pockets, leaned her shoulder against the truck's camper shell, and looked fondly at her daughter. "Since you seem to be in charge, what do you want me to do?"

"Well..." Ann wrinkled her forehead thoughtfully, then the dimples cracked in her cheeks. "You can take Dr. Conover up and show him the waterfall."

"I could start cutting vegetables."

"No, Mom. Really. Just take a hike or something."

Bryant chuckled. "Take a hike?"

Deborah glanced at him with a sudden grin, then swung back to Ann. "I'm sure there must be something I can do to help."

Ann propped her hands on her hips. "You can get out of my hair."

Deborah lifted her hands in defeat. "Okay, okay. If you need me, call." Turning to Bryant, she shrugged. "I know you're just dying to see this waterfall."

"I guess I am."

"I love a man who's game for adventure." The words came naturally, without thought. The way someone would say they love pizza or opera. Bryant wished he could accept them the same way, but something about them made it personal. Which was absurd. He and Deborah were chaperons, the parents of these children. She turned toward the creek, and he had no choice but to follow.

Without a trail, they clambered over rocks and around thick stands of brush. Patches of ice brightened the shadows, and once they were out of the direct sun the breeze felt cool on Bryant's face. Splashing noisily along its rocky bed, the creek smelled of melted snow.

Deborah didn't seem troubled by the rugged terrain. She moved as surely as some wild, graceful animal, over a rock, around a bush, across a patch of ice. And her jeans molded to her as if they'd been woven to fit, with her hips and thighs defined by denim like a Madison Avenue ad.

He had to watch her to know how to go, and watching her did strange things to his physiology. Normal body functions, such as the heart sending blood through the veins and the lungs regulating air flow, seemed to lose the patterns of a lifetime.

Stopping abruptly, she pivoted with the grace and speed of a deer to face him. He stumbled on the uneven footing and teetered toward her. As if to catch him, her hands pressed against his chest.

"Careful. I guess I didn't realize you were so close."

Her touch burned through his jacket, his shirt, his flesh. Through the shadows, a stray beam of light touched her cheek. Her eyes danced like the sparkles of sun on the rushing water beside them.

He wanted her.

The realization came hot and fierce. It leapt and growled against his instant effort to restrain it. She'd started burrowing into his mind and under his skin the first moment he'd seen her. She heated his blood and blocked out reason.

Without thinking, he touched his lips to hers. Warm and soft, sweet as sunlight. He pulled her closer and deepened the kiss. This was life. Ancient forest, the sky and the breeze, the silence broken only by the song of the water. A man and a woman.

Her lips moved, responded. The hands on his chest slipped around to his back, urging him closer. Oh, yes. Her body fit against his like two puzzle pieces coming together. He could feel her heart beating in time with his. He wanted to wrap her closer, press her head against his shoulder, drink in the fresh scent of her and never let go.

Suddenly, shakily, Deborah pushed away. "No. This is not a good idea." Her voice sounded low, breathless, uncertain.

Effective. Bryant let his hands fall to his side and backed away. "You're right, it's a terrible idea." But having tasted the forbidden fruit, how could he forget?

He fought to keep the situation in perspective. Otherwise, his baser instincts and the mood of the glen might influence him to unbutton her shirt, unfasten her belt and lie with her there in the first new grass of spring.

For the first time, Deborah wished her daughters were neither competent nor efficient. If she'd been able to watch the fire, or tend the Dutch-oven peach cobbler, or keep the shier kids involved, she wouldn't have been able to think about Bryant. But no, between them Ann and Lane engineered the entire meal.

And they made sure all their friends stayed busy, leaving her nothing to do but relive a kiss. Over and over again.

Maybe if Bryant's eyes weren't the color of lichen on granite, shades of green and gray mixed together, she could have focused on something else. Maybe if when they met hers, her equilibrium didn't teeter dangerously. Maybe if she could turn back the clock about six months and not send one of her letters to Conover Memorial in Milwaukee. Unfortunately, she had to live with current reality.

And the truth was, she'd enjoyed kissing him. And hated it.

A part of her felt like a teenager again. Lightheaded, giddy, irresponsible. Another deeper part ached for Jay, for all the years they might have had together. Once, long ago, she'd loved with the intensity of youth and the power of forever. For thirteen years she'd kept Jay in her heart, like the best part of herself. Now, for another man, her pulse raced with recklessness.

Confusion clouded her wisdom. She felt like flirting with Bryant, maybe even teasing him into kissing her again. Cautiously, she let her eyes drift in his direction. He sat on a rock, trying to follow Lane's instructions on how to turn his foil-wrapped dinner on the coals. He looked like somebody's conception of the ideal man. Smooth good looks, gorgeous body, dangerous smile. Today, after a couple of hours outdoors, his dark blond hair had lost its just combed look, and a lock fell rakishly across his forehead.

Damn. Longing stirred deep within her, and Deborah sucked her bottom lip between her teeth.

She had to get this feeling under control. She wasn't a girl anymore. She was a mother, a responsible adult, a one-man woman. She had the ability to look at the future and foresee the consequences. But there was no way on earth she could avoid being around Bryant Conover. Not today, and not for the rest of his stay.

So she had two choices. She could put that little, nothing kiss in perspective, realizing her emotions were her own to control. Or she could let it hang between them, making all future contact awkward.

Any reasonable person—and she had always been reasonable—would insist on the first course of action. Especially since he'd only been in town a week and had a full year to go.

She watched him push his food packet around in the coals until it wedged against a rock. When he finally managed to flip it over, Lane clapped approval.

He looked like a kid hooking his first fish, satisfied and eager. When his eyes met Deborah's, she stopped breathing. Controlling her emotions was one thing; controlling her reaction to him was going to be quite another.

Before they finished eating, Ann started talking about a hike to Lake Thompson. Immediately Lane joined in, and Scott, who'd also been there before, called it one of the best places around.

Since all the kids had jackets, Deborah let the plan develop. Here in the sun, sheltered from the wind by the curve of the mountain, the day felt almost like early summer. Up higher, they'd be reminded it was only late April.

"How far is it?" Mary Margaret asked in her gentle voice. Deborah knew from past experience that she preferred to avoid physical activity whenever possible. Because of that, it was always a surprise when the twins wanted to include her.

"About a mile and a half," Lane said.

"But it's not at all steep," Ann added, making it sound like an easy walk to the store.

Nathan, who'd been hanging close to Mary Margaret all afternoon, grinned at her and winked. "You can set the pace."

Grabbing Matt's hand, Lane pulled him more firmly into the circle. "You'll love this lake. It's so blue it looks like a reflection of the sky, and so clear you think the water's clean enough to drink."

"Isn't it?" Matt asked in surprise.

The sound of his voice startled Deborah, and she realized in chagrin that he'd hardly spoken at all since they arrived. She'd been too preoccupied with his father to even notice.

Lane laughed. "*No* water is safe unless you purify it."

As sensitive as Matt was, Deborah thought he'd withdraw from Lane, with her laughter and her note of superiority. But he only shrugged. "We have lakes back home. And you don't have to hike a mile to get to them."

"I like hiking," Jessica cut in defensively. "When you get up in the mountains, the sky seems so close you could touch it."

Matt made a rude noise, but Lane laughed before anyone could take offense and the mood stayed light. "See for yourself." Her stance and tone of voice made it a challenge.

Matt met it straight on. "Sure." His chin stuck out aggressively, even though the faintest hint of a grin pulled at one side of his mouth. He reminded Deborah of a swaggering punk kid straight out of *West Side Story*.

Ann turned to Bryant. "You want to come, don't you? It's a great place."

Deborah knew that if the kids went, she and Bryant would have to go, too. Not necessarily to chaperon, but to avoid being alone with each other, waiting.

"I don't think these are the right kind of shoes," he said, looking down at them.

Since they had smooth leather soles, Deborah didn't think they were either, but both Lane and Ann jumped in to reassure him he'd do fine.

"Unless there's snow on the trail," Deborah murmured to herself. Any northern exposure was likely to have remaining patches. She imagined Bryant sprawled on an ice field. Unhurt, of course. But she would come to his aid, steadying him as he scrambled back on his feet, his arm around her shoulder and her hand on his chest—

"What?" Bryant asked.

She whipped her eyes to his. Surely, he hadn't read her thoughts. No, they were talking about his shoes. She had to get a grip. Stay logical. Start acting her age.

It felt like a sentence. Twelve months to go, and it looked as if she'd have to start marking off days on a calendar. As a doctor, she would like for him to stay forever. As a man, she would have no peace of mind until he left.

Chapter Four

It was not much bigger than the pond behind Deborah's house, and Bryant decided that on its own merits Lake Thompson would be a joke.

Located in the bowl of the mountain, with a barren, jagged peak rising dramatically above it, it looked like a piece of liquid mirror poured onto the ground. Several stands of pine arrowed down toward it, while to the south an ancient rockslide left a swath of boulders like a gray lava flow sweeping down the slope. Patches of snow brightened the shadows, and ice still covered the northernmost third of the lake.

Out in the open, the wind felt a little too brisk for comfort. Even the sun, slanting from the west, didn't quite cut the chill. While everyone milled around on the bank of the lake, he climbed on top of a car-size boulder to catch any heat stored in the rock.

It didn't surprise him that Deborah kept herself surrounded by the teenagers. That kiss at the waterfall had unsettled her. Maybe even frightened her. It had sure as hell torn him from his moorings. He should probably be glad she'd pulled away. He had come to Sterling to reclaim his son, not plunge into an infatuation. But he couldn't stop watching her, or listening for her rippling laughter to rise above the babble of the group. He found himself looking at her far too frequently, expecting to meet her eyes, to share without words his reaction to what was happening around them.

A rock skipped across the water and caught his attention. It hopped three times before sinking. On the bank, Lane stood sideways to the lake, her face serious with concentration. She leaned forward slightly at the waist, swung her arm back, took three steps and let the rock fly. Five hops, five rings that widened and wove into each other. The kids cheered and she whooped with success.

Deborah edged forward, laughing and shouldering people out of the way. The kids gave her plenty of room to make her throw. Fascinated, Bryant watched her caress a stone to get the feel of it. With the calculated approach of a big-league pitcher, she sent the rock gliding parallel to the water's surface. Twenty feet from the bank it touched down and sank. She groaned in disappointment while the group laughed.

After that it became a free-for-all. Even Matt tried his skill. To Bryant's surprise and satisfaction, his son didn't stomp away when his first attempt failed. Or his second and third. Perhaps it was Lane's doing. She showed him how to find the right shape of stone, then how to hurl it across the water, concentrating on wrist action. Each time his rock sank, she encouraged him to try again. Long after the others had drifted away toward the boulder flow, Matt continued until he finally got two jumps in a row.

Silently cheering Matt's success, Bryant watched the rapport growing between his son and Lane and compared it to how Matt had been in Milwaukee. Mostly Matt had kept himself isolated, never bringing friends home or spending time on the telephone. Until a couple of months ago. Then he suddenly began staying out for long periods of time, often not coming home until one or two in the morning. He started cutting school. He got picked up for shoplifting. When Bryant noticed the first telltale signs of drug use, he decided some changes had to be made.

He put Matt in counseling and considered tougher measures such as private hospitals with drug programs or survival expeditions for troubled teens. Then Deborah Pingree's invitation landed on his desk, and Bryant decided that working with his son to solve their problems together held more promise than sending Matt off to fight his demons alone.

Today might not be as "together" as Bryant would have liked, but Matt seemed less angry than at any time since Nikki had sent him to Milwaukee.

By the time Matt and Lane gave up skipping rocks, the other kids had drifted around the lake to the boulder field. More content than he'd been in years, Bryant linked his hands behind his head and lay back on the rock. The heat soon penetrated his sweater and shirt, relaxing him, and he closed his eyes. It felt good to let go for a few minutes and not worry.

Then someone pulled on his foot.

"Time to join the party. We're going bouldering."

He sat up to find Deborah grinning at him. The sun backlit the fine, flyaway strands of hair that had come loose from her braid. Her nose hinted at a touch of burn. Her smile made the breath catch in his throat.

He levered onto his elbows, and the clear blue of her eyes hit him in the heart with the force of a sledge-hammer. Firmly, he banked down the fire and kept any sign of it from his voice. "What if I'd rather stay here?"

"You can. But it won't be fun." She pointed toward the others, and he followed the direction of her hand.

Evidently, bouldering meant hopping from one rock to another. It was the kind of thing teenagers should be doing, participating as a group, being outdoors, testing their bodies in new situations. It was something he hadn't been able to give Matt. Hell, he hadn't had it himself. By his tenth birthday he'd decided to be a doctor. All through school he had loaded himself with math and science classes, graduating early and CLEP-testing himself out of enough subjects to jump straight into premed work.

Until now he had never considered what he'd missed. The decision to come to Montana kept taking on new dimensions.

"I could wait for you to come back."

Deborah laughed, and the sound of it lifted into the breeze the way a flute accents an orchestra. "We won't be back. We'll follow the flow to the bottom, then cut across to the truck. Come on, you'll like it."

"My shoes—"

"Aren't a problem. Not on a flow this old and settled. New avalanches can be treacherous, but you'll be fine here if you watch your step."

Unconvinced, but willing to try, he slid off the rock. He'd looked to the mountains for answers, he might as well start here. Deborah tipped her head in the direction they should go, and stayed a good arm's length apart from him—as though she knew he wanted to touch her. As though she could read in his eyes how much he wanted to kiss her again.

Within minutes of starting down the boulder flow, Bryant knew that unless the others waited for them at some point, they'd never catch up. Every rock was a different size, at a different angle, lodged a different distance from its neighbor, with pockets of ice filling most of the shadows. Deborah hopped from one to another like a mountain goat, while Bryant didn't trust his ability to judge his next step. At least they were going down, which he assumed required less effort than climbing up.

Below them, he had a clear view of the kids. Matt and Lane made good time and quickly caught up with Mary Margaret, Jessica and Nathan. Below them, Ann and Scott widened the gap.

With a flash of optimism, Bryant watched the way Matt interacted with the others. If any outside influence could help his son, this environment was it. If any group of people could help restore Matt's self-esteem, the Pingrees and their friends were those people. Suddenly, the politics and strategies that had been important to him at Conover Memorial seemed too distant to matter. The concern his father and grandfather shared, that leaving the hospital even for a year would destroy his future, lost immediacy.

Of course, he and Matt still had a long way to go. Any fool could see that. The boy hardly talked to him, let alone confided in him or considered him a friend. But hopefully, that would come later. In the meantime—

"Oh, God. Something's the matter. Hurry!"

Deborah grabbed his hand, practically jerking him down the slope. Even as he pulled himself out of his reverie, her urgency gripped him. Below, he saw the kids in a huddle, but he could discern no details.

"What is it?"

"I don't know. Look at Lane. She's scared." Deborah's voice trembled and her hand turned damp in his as she hurried him along.

Adrenaline surged through his body. His feet found their way over the boulders as if guided by an unseen force. He almost kept up with Deborah.

When they got closer, the kids' anxious cries began to separate into individual voices.

"Where's the first-aid kit?" Lane demanded. "Who's got it?"

"Is he going to be all right?"

"It happened so fast. All of a sudden he just slipped."

Then Matt's voice, hoarse and shaky, rose above the rest. "My dad! He's a doctor."

My dad. The words hit Bryant with an impact that took his breath away. Not once in fifteen years had he heard them from Matt. But he didn't have time to savor them.

Deborah reached the group first, and the kids opened a way for her and Bryant. Nathan lay awkwardly on the uneven rocks, his flesh deadly white. With her face nearly as pale as his, she dropped beside the boy. When Bryant knelt next to her, she glanced up briefly.

"His head's split open. Ann, the first-aid kit."

"I don't have it, Mom."

"Oh, God." Pulling her sweatshirt over her head and turning it inside out at the same time, Deborah pressed a clean section against Nathan's head. Without a word, Ann took out a pocketknife and ripped into the other side of the sweatshirt, being careful not to disturb the section that Deborah held tight to Nathan's injury.

Deborah handled the emergency smoothly, but when her eyes flicked to Bryant's, the distress in them stunned him. She radiated panic, from the tight line of her mouth to the hunch of her shoulders. He eased in to take over, amazed she could apply enough pressure to the wound with her hand shaking so badly.

He lifted the scrap of shirt to examine the wound. Blood covered the boy's forehead and dripped onto the rock, but the flow had slowed.

"Do we have water?" he asked.

"No." Held-back tears cracked Deborah's voice.

More than once while assisting a surgeon in the operating room, Bryant had found his mind functioning on multiple levels. While concern for the patient came first, he'd still been able to hear the comments of attending personnel, hear the bells and announcements on the intercom, note any minute temperature changes in the room. Now he experienced the same phenomenon with Deborah. With his full attention on Nathan, he felt her tension inch toward the breaking point.

He cleaned Nathan's injury as well as he could with a second piece of the sweatshirt. Handing it to him, Deborah's hand still trembled.

"It's not deep," Bryant told her, and her relief hung tangibly between them. "Because they bleed so much, head wounds often seem worse than they are."

From the rest of the sweatshirt, he fashioned a bandage that would work until they got back to his office. Before he let Nathan sit up, he checked for broken bones and ran a couple of quick tests for concussion. So far he'd seen nothing to indicate a serious injury, but some symptoms didn't show up right away.

When he backed away, at least six pairs of hands assisted Nathan to his feet.

With a grin, Nathan shrugged away their help. "Hey, I'm okay. You don't need to act like I'm dead." He looped his arm around Mary Margaret's shoulders, even though it seemed likely he could manage on his own.

"There are only two ways to get back on the trail," Deborah said tightly. "Back up, or on down. Believe me, down is easier."

Bryant nodded. "Then down it is."

Out of consideration for Nathan, everyone went more slowly the rest of the way. There was a little jockeying of position to see who would flank him, and Scott and Mary Margaret won. With the emergency over, Matt edged away from the group again. But he didn't go alone, Lane stayed with him, bridging the distance he still couldn't bring himself to close.

Bryant knew he shouldn't revel in someone else's misfortune. But since Nathan hadn't been seriously injured, gratitude and new hope rose within him.

My dad. The words resonated through his brain like a mantra. Things would be all right. Things would get better. How could he not feel optimistic?

Dividing his attention between Matt and Nathan, it was five or ten minutes before Bryant noticed that Deborah held back from the group. She watched Nathan with such a grim expression he suspected something stronger than concern for the boy troubled her. He remembered her reaction to the accident.

This woman ran a school that took people into the mountains. She obviously knew how to handle emergencies. She probably had a Red Cross card. But in applying first aid to Nathan's head, she'd been as shaky as a leaf in a windstorm. Something didn't add up.

He let her draw even with him and crossed the boulders that separated them. "Are you all right?"

She turned in surprise. "Sure."

He saw the lie in her eyes. "No, you're not. What's the matter?"

"Nothing."

"He's going to be okay."

"Yes. Thank you, doctor."

He caught her arm to make her stop. "If I hadn't been here, you'd have managed just fine."

"My first-aid kit's in the truck— No, it isn't. It's home in my car. I didn't even bring a canteen. Mistakes like that could be fatal. Don't tell me I would have managed."

"You would have. The injury wasn't all that bad."

"And what if it had been worse? What if—" Her voice broke and she swung away.

"What if, what?"

"Nothing. We'd better go. They're getting too far ahead."

Her pain cut deep, deeper than a scratch on the head warranted. His hands wanted to pull her close, his arms wanted to hold her. He wanted to tap the well and let it flood over, until whatever troubled her drained away.

But she'd already outpaced him. With the deftness of experience, she jumped from boulder to boulder until he knew he couldn't catch her without putting his own neck at risk.

Deborah drove straight to Bryant's office. With Nathan in the front seat between them, acting nothing like a casualty, there had been little opportunity for conversation. Thank goodness. She couldn't stop Bryant from watching her with that numbing intensity, but at least he couldn't ask her any questions.

On the other hand, she couldn't ask him any either. And she desperately wanted to know if he sensed how important he was to the community. Of course, any doctor would do. But she didn't have just any doctor. She had him.

Coming to a slow stop, out of consideration for a patient who probably didn't notice, Deborah turned in the seat and met Bryant's eyes. Could she impress him with the urgency she felt? Would it make any difference? He'd contracted for a year. She wanted him forever.

"I'll take the kids home and be back," she said.

Bryant hesitated, shrugged and got out. Nathan twisted in the seat and banged on the cab window to catch the attention of the kids in the back, then he opened his mouth and pressed his face, including his tongue, against the glass.

"How gross," Deborah groaned, trying not to laugh. Nathan would be fine and life would go on. "Plan on washing that window when I get back."

"It'd probably pull out my stitches," he objected.

"Not a chance," Bryant said. He took Nathan's arm and urged him out of the truck. Over Nathan's head, his eyes locked with Deborah's again. "I predict he's going to be fine."

"I bow to your professional opinion. Nathan, if you want, I can call your mom."

Bryant shook his head. "We shouldn't wait for you. I'll call her."

"I better do it." For the first time since leaving Moose Flats, Nathan looked slightly abashed. "If you call her, she'll think I'm really hurt."

"We wouldn't want that."

Bryant pushed the door shut, and Deborah shifted into gear with a sigh of relief. She felt calmer. Almost normal. After thirteen years, the fear no longer immobilized her. But it still took conscious effort to separate images in her mind. Few of the injuries they dealt with through the wilderness school affected her, even when they were miles and hours from help. Unless there was blood. Then the memory rushed back, imposing itself over reality. Always, she saw Jay.

But she *could* separate them. She could think of what to do and do it. So what if, afterward, she wanted to go off by herself and curl into a ball? This time there had been a doctor on the spot. This time had been relatively easy.

Deborah delivered the friends to their homes, then drove to the Merc to leave the truck and pick up her car. When Lane asked if they could get Cokes, she left her big ring of keys with the twins and Matt and walked back up the hill to Bryant's office.

Bryant, Nathan and Nathan's mother, Myra Enger, were all in the waiting room. Nathan had a neat square bandage taped onto the side of his forehead just below the hairline.

"Hey, Debbie, can you believe this kid of mine?" Myra began, the minute Deborah walked in the door. "Falling like some two-year-old. When do they grow out of being clumsy? Dr. Conover here's been so good to tell me it wasn't anyone's fault, that they were just having a good time. I think it serves him right for being rowdy, don't you?" She turned to Nathan and brushed his hair off his forehead, skimming so close to the bandage Deborah winced. "Or were you showing off for the girls? Maybe you learned a lesson."

"They weren't being rowdy," Deborah said. "It could have happened to any of them. Of course, it did get him a little attention of the right kind." She winked at Nathan and he winked back.

"Well, whatever," Myra went on. "At least the doctor was right there. I can't tell you how secure it makes me feel to know I don't have to worry about a thing. And we don't have to drive all the way into Bozeman. If we did, Nathan would probably fall asleep on the way, and I'd be worrying about a concussion or something and thinking I should be trying to keep him awake."

Deborah remembered how hard it had been to convince Nathan to ride up front with her and Bryant, instead of in the back—where the rest of the kids had been *very* rowdy. And she remembered the smear on her window, which she couldn't make him wash off because the truck was now at the Merc.

"I'm glad we can reassure you," Bryant said. "Nathan is fine. There's no reason he can't go to school tomorrow."

Myra smothered Bryant with thanks and praise for at least five more minutes before Nathan practically pulled her out the door.

As soon as it closed behind them, Bryant began to laugh. "She's incredible."

"That's one word for it," Deborah agreed. "Are you ready to go home? I left our children at the store guzzling pop."

"Then they'll be fine for a few more minutes."

"Sure. Do you need to finish up some pa—" Her eyes met his, and the moment of humor inspired by Myra Enger ebbed away.

"What happened on the mountain, Deborah?"

She should have seen it coming. She should have planned what to say. "Nathan cracked his head open."

"What else?"

"Our doctor fixed him up. A milestone. Something that couldn't have happened last year, or the year before, or at any time in the past fifteen years. A cause for celebration, don't you think?"

He caught her by the shoulders. "Be straight with me."

"Look, you came to Sterling and were here to sew up Nathan's head. That's significant. We all appreciate you. We hope you know how important you are."

"It wasn't gratitude you felt on the mountain. It was fear, or guilt. Or maybe a little of both."

Deborah broke free of his grip and put the width of the room between them. Wrapping her arms across her chest, she faced him. "You can't possibly know what it's like. Medical care has probably been only a phone call away your entire life. Here, the distance is sometimes a matter of life and death.

"Do you think people in Milwaukee *deserve* that advantage? Or that they earned it? No, it just happened because of where they live. But *I* want the security of knowing my mother's health is never jeopardized if I can't get her to Bozeman in the middle of winter, or that if a baby decides to come too soon someone qualified will be there to deliver it, or that a cold can get diagnosed before it turns into pneumonia. Is that asking too much?"

"I'll be here a year."

She swung away and leaned her shoulder against the window frame. "I know. Thank you." She hadn't gotten this much of a commitment before, but she knew she would never stop looking for a total, complete, permanent solution.

"That's all you asked for."

Hearing the challenge in his voice, she turned back to him. Could he read her so easily? Did he know how hard it had been to compromise her aspirations for the sake of getting anyone at all? "It's all I *dared* ask for. It's not all I want."

He crossed the room and took a position at the other side of the window. Late afternoon sun streamed between them, creating an elongated grid of light on the tile floor. He held her eyes across a path of shimmering dust motes.

"I'm in line to become the next chief of family medicine at Conover Memorial. Every career move I've made since entering medical school has focused on achieving that position. My family thinks I'm crazy to be here at all."

"So why did you come?"

A flow of emotions she couldn't read played across his face before he shook his head. "I intend to fulfill the terms of my contract."

"Then we understand each other."

He took a step closer. The sun lit his hair and turned his eyes to pools dark with meaning. "I don't think we do. The riddle of what happened on the mountain remains unanswered."

Her heart hammered painfully in her chest as the heat of his gaze poured through her. When she tried to speak, the words caught in her throat. "Maybe it has no answer."

"I think it does."

Hours had passed since their kiss in the woods. Laughter and drama, worry and fear had filled the minutes and turned the tide of her thoughts. Now it all came rushing back. The warmth of his lips, the strength of his arms, the soaring hunger to experience it again. But older memories wove through present emotions until she couldn't tell them apart. How much of her reaction to Bryant came from missing Jay so much for so long?

Taking a deep breath, she forced a smile. Inside she was nearly as unsteady and frightened as when Nathan had been lying in a pool of his own blood. But this time, she knew she could keep it from showing. "Want a Coke?"

With a quick shake of his head, he laughed wryly. "Why do I suspect that's all I'll get from you today?"

"Because you're very astute."

"And you're very prudent."

"I have to be."

He switched off the lights and held the door for her. As she brushed past him, she felt the warmth of his body and the jump of her nerves. She ignored both.

Friday morning, Deborah saw Bryant's car in his driveway when she left for work. Normally he left early enough to drive Matt to school, so she considered going over to see if everything was all right.

She fought the impulse and backed down the drive without glancing at his house again. If he needed her, he'd have called. And if he didn't need her, she'd be a fool to jump to conclusions. The past five days had been difficult enough without inviting trouble.

All week she'd kept running into Bryant. At the bank, in the drugstore, on the street. He came into the Merc every evening to pick up Matt, and most days more often than that. For groceries. For snacks to stock the refrigerator at his clinic. To talk.

And she'd enjoyed every minute in his company.

But her reactions to him didn't feel like friendship. If Glen walked into the room, her heart didn't rise to her throat. When Sam O'Roark said her name, flashes of pleasure didn't sing through her mind. Sometimes Charlie hitched his hip onto the corner of her desk, but it never shot her brain into fantasy overdrive.

On the other hand, what besides friendship could it be? Infatuation, maybe, although that seemed more a teen thing. Physical attraction? Goodness knows her celibate life left her wide open for it. More likely, she just wasn't used to male attention and didn't have the skills to deal with it.

Well, it was time to gain them. She couldn't spend an entire year turning to mush every time Bryant Conover entered the room. And what better time than the present? She certainly didn't need to worry about why he might be off schedule.

The blast of a horn blared through the mountain silence, and she swerved in time to avoid sideswiping a rusty pickup. Waving a sheepish apology to Orvill Peterson, she sucked in a deep breath. Obviously, she'd allowed the good doctor to have too big a share of her thoughts.

At the store, she spent twenty minutes discussing a late shipment of alfalfa seed with Charlie, then buried herself in paperwork. Orders, invoices, bills, payroll, those were the only things she would allow herself to think about.

When the phone rang, she jumped. It rang again before she got to it. "Hello?"

"Debbie? This is Shirley. Have you seen Dr. Conover today? He hasn't gotten in yet, and he's never late. I keep worrying that something might have happened to him. I called his house, but there was no answer, so I thought I'd check with you."

"Why? I haven't seen him at all."

"Oh. Living next door, you know, I thought you'd know if something was wrong."

Of course. Deborah sighed with relief. Neighbors usually kept tabs on each other. It was nothing more than that.

"And you've been seeing so much of him," Shirley continued, "I thought if something *had* come up, he'd certainly have told *you.*"

"No. He wouldn't have."

Just then Bryant's Saab went past the store, up the road toward his office. Deborah experienced a totally different kind of relief. He wasn't ill, he wasn't hurt, nothing tragic had happened. "Shirley, he just drove by. He should be there any second."

"Well, thank heavens for that. You can't imagine. I just kept thinking the worst, and the later it got the more worried I got. He's so dedicated, you know, always here right on time, always willing to see people, even if they didn't make an appointment first. And he

makes people feel like they got their money's worth,
even if there wasn't anything much wrong with them.
I've seen it happen over and over again. Oh, here he
is. He just drove up. Well, I'm so relieved, I can't tell
you. Listen, I've got to go. Please tell your mother
hello for me. I know I need to get over and see her
more often, but— Good morning, Dr. Conover. Bye,
Debbie, it was so nice visiting with you.''

"Yes, it was,'' Deborah said to the abruptly silent
phone. She could almost hear Shirley rattling on to
Bryant without a breath, going on about how sure she
was Debbie would have known where he was, since
they spent so much time together.

As if Deborah needed a good, solid reason to stick
to her decision to avoid him. It was obviously no
longer a matter of congenial community gossip. Once
people started making assumptions and acting as if a
thing were fact, the truth didn't matter anymore.
Every year a couple of high school kids ended up getting married, just because the expectations of others
got too strong for them to resist.

She couldn't let Bryant walk onto that kind of mine
field.

Of course, she and Bryant weren't kids, and Bryant
probably wouldn't bow to public opinion any more
than she would. But he didn't need the hassle, and
Matt didn't need to be hounded by insinuations.

So Dr. Conover was now on his own. No more long
chats out on the street. No more cookouts. No more
coffee breaks with his feet propped on her desk. At
least his constant presence hadn't yet developed into
a habit she couldn't break.

Chapter Five

Jeans, hiking boots, heavy socks, compass, canteen. Bryant had a list tucked in his pocket, but the items ran through his head like a litany.

He pushed through the Merc's double swinging doors and immediately looked to Deborah's office. Built a few feet above floor level so she could look out over the store, it drew his eyes first whenever he came here. Today she wasn't at her desk. For a heartbeat disappointment flared, even though he knew he'd probably find her soon if he wandered up and down the aisles.

Of all the reasons he'd come to Montana, the possibility of finding himself caught in a woman's spell had not crossed his mind. But Deborah's lack of guile and her indifference to her own appeal fascinated him. He'd never known anyone like her, and he couldn't make himself stay away.

At least today he had a solid reason for seeking her out. He needed help.

Since the cookout at Moose Flats, Matt had grown more and more impossible. The brief moment of hope when he'd heard Matt say *my dad,* had disappeared faster than an ice cube in boiling water. His every effort to open lines of communication had ended in failure, reaching a new low this morning.

When he'd suggested they hike to one of the nearby mountains, Matt had expressed his disgust for the idea in graphic terms. Bryant had tried to reason past Matt's objections, which had only fueled the boy's rebellion. The argument had turned into a battle, which made Matt late for school and Bryant even later for work.

Bryant knew Matt had one or two legitimate points. Neither of them owned the right clothing or equipment, and Bryant didn't know enough about the mountains to be a good follower, let alone a guide.

Matt also made a lot of stupid, illogical points, but Bryant couldn't do anything about them. He *could* get better prepared. So he'd come to the most accomplished person he knew for help.

He found her in the warehouse, clearing a big chunk of floor space. Charlie ran a small forklift while Deborah wrote something on a clipboard.

During the past week he'd noticed that she usually bound her hair into a braid for work. Today she'd fixed a little yellow bow on the end to match her T-shirt, with a pencil she'd obviously forgotten sticking out of it at an angle. She always wore her shirts tucked in, and too often his hands itched to test the span of her waist.

When he stepped deeper into the room, she glanced up. Her eyes darkened for the briefest of seconds, and her smile followed slowly. Always before, she'd welcomed him without hesitation. Had something changed since yesterday?

With a wave she signaled him to wait while she directed Charlie where to unload a stack of bulging gunnysacks. She talked to Charlie for a couple of minutes, gesturing with her hands, then tucked her clipboard under her arm.

Something *had* changed since yesterday. Bryant saw it in her slow step and the way she twisted her pencil through her fingers. Trouble here at the store? Something wrong with her mother? Or the twins? But if it were medical, she'd have come immediately to him.

She didn't try to speak until she got close enough to be heard above the forklift engine.

"Hi." Her smile still didn't reach her eyes.

"I've come begging."

That brought her natural laughter bubbling to the surface. Obviously the problem didn't run too deep.

"Don't you need an eye patch for that? Or at least a phony cane?"

Her ready response, in spite of whatever troubled her, unknotted a strand of his worry about Matt. "Not alms. Help and advice."

Arching her straight eyebrows, she let the laughter fade away. "Advice?"

He lifted his hands in surrender, since he'd rejected her initial efforts to help. "Please don't hold past mistakes against me. Or past judgments. For this problem, I know you're the best source of information."

The forklift shifted gears and the engine revved, echoing through the cavernous warehouse.

"Come on." She tipped her head toward the doors and indicated he should go first. "Let's go where we don't have to yell."

She didn't lead him to her office, or ask him if he'd like something to drink. Instead, she paused in the middle of an aisle and kept a distance between them he hadn't noticed before. Maybe her hesitation concerned him, and not some other kind of problem. If he'd offended her, he couldn't think when. All week she'd been open and welcoming, and he'd responded like dry grass to a good downpour.

And with about as much reserve, he admitted silently. Maybe he'd been too friendly without realizing it. Okay. Fine. If she wanted distance, he'd be happy to oblige.

"I want to take Matt hiking this weekend. We need the right kind of shoes, and maybe some maps or something."

Her quick smile killed all thought of distance. It invited him to relax with her, to be friends.

"Sure. Do you want to start with boots?"

"I guess."

She headed down the aisle and he followed, wondering what it was about her. Her willingness maybe. Or her self-assurance. Or the way she could reach out without a word. Whatever, she made him believe in possibilities.

By the time she'd fitted him with a good hiking boot, Bryant had conquered the hurt and frustration left over from his argument with Matt. He'd get the equipment he needed and find a starting point.

Deborah sat on her heels and wedged his new boots back in the box. "What else?"

"You tell me—you're the expert."

"Jeans."

He straightened the crease on his slacks and shook his head ruefully. "I haven't owned jeans since junior high school."

"Bryant!"

The shock in her voice made him chuckle. Jeans probably made her world possible, where people earned their living with sweat and calluses. "Doctors don't need them, and I knew I'd be a doctor before I turned ten."

"Come on. Ten?"

"It was my destiny. My father's chief of surgery at Conover Memorial, my grandfather's chief of staff. My great-grandfather endowed the hospital, and as I told you I'm next in line to be chief of family medicine when the position comes open in about two years."

"Dr. M. Bryant Conover III." She set the boots aside and started toward the shelves of Levi's at the back of the store. Turning to look at him over her shoulder, she let the words linger on her tongue. "Does the M stand for Matthew?"

"That's my grandfather's name. My father goes by M.B."

"And your son is Matthew Bryant Conover IV?"

If her eyes hadn't been growing steadily lighter with humor, he might have resented the path of her thoughts. Instead he met her grin with one of his own. "You want to make a federal case of it?"

"Poor Matt. I believe in family, but that's a little extreme, don't you think? Didn't your wife object?"

"Actually, she did. I got around her by filling out the birth certificate and signing it before anyone asked her."

"At Conover Memorial Hospital."

"Where else would my son be born?"

"I'll bet she loved you for going behind her back."

"No, but for a lot of reasons stronger than that one." Suddenly it wasn't funny anymore. Hundreds of little things had added up to the failure of his marriage. Naming Matt over Nikki's objections actually came way down on the list of his personal contributions. "I wasn't much of a husband."

Deborah handed him a pair of indigo jeans and studied him thoughtfully. He wondered what she hoped to understand. How he'd failed? Why? The reasons he wasn't much of a father now?

When she spoke, her voice carried more sympathy than he deserved. "I'm sure you did the best you could."

"No. I was finishing my residency, and I cared about being a good doctor more than I cared about her. After she took Matt away, it was easy to bury myself in my work."

"How old was Matt?"

"Just over a year. I didn't see him again until ten months ago."

Her hand flew to her chest and all light left her eyes. "Bryant, no! She kept him from you?"

He'd never discussed it with anyone, not even his father. The pain had cut too deep for words, too sharp for comfort. He could accept his own culpability in ruining his marriage, but he'd never understood Nikki's need to hurt him by hiding Matt so thoroughly.

For the first time in fourteen years, he found himself wanting to cauterize the wound with words.

"She arranged for me to send support checks to her lawyer, but she never held up her end by allowing visitation. I tried to keep track of her, but she moved too frequently for me to see Matt. It was almost as though she had ESP. One day we'd know her address, where she worked, where she banked, even where she shopped for groceries. The next day she'd be gone. Eight months or a year later, I'd locate her again."

"It must have been hell."

"I used to lie awake nights plotting how to get him back from her." Once he'd even flown to Baton Rouge, intent on finding Matt and bringing him home before Nikki knew to whisk him away again. Carrying a picture of Matt taken by a private investigator, he'd spent an entire day watching children go in and out of an elementary school. But he hadn't been able to pick his son out of the hundreds of boys. That night one of his patients had been admitted to the hospital with a ruptured tubal pregnancy, and he'd rushed home without knowing whether he would have had the will to follow through anyway. To Matt, he'd have been a stranger, a threat, taking him from the only security he knew. When Nikki moved again within a week, he lost the chance to try again.

Pressure on his arm broke the painful direction of his memories. When he glanced down, he saw Deborah's hand, small and strong and uncompromising, offering comfort where there had been only unhappiness.

"He's yours now. And you love him."

"But he hates me."

"You'll find a way to break through."

"Or die trying."

"It will hardly come to that." With a little squeeze and a smile, she made him feel hopeful again. This morning's argument with Matt still prickled, but it no longer weighed him down.

Deborah ached for Bryant. She'd experienced loss. She knew how it felt. But her losses had always been final. She'd been able to grieve, recover and go on. She tried to imagine the emptiness of knowing his son existed, somewhere out of reach. He'd missed Matt's first steps, his first words, his first day of school. He'd missed the discovery of talents, the impatience over food preferences, the closeness of a bedtime story. He must have worried constantly about the boy growing up without a father, moving too frequently from one place to another to have any roots. He couldn't have known, but must have imagined, the stories his ex-wife told his son about him.

Evidently, those stories had been potent. And negative. Why else would Matt feel so much anger toward Bryant? If Deborah had been anxious to help him before, now she knew she'd be unable to back away. Maybe she wouldn't be able to help bridge the chasm, but she could lend a sympathetic ear. So what if gossips like Shirley jumped to conclusions? So what if word got out that she and Bryant spent a lot of time together? What did rumors matter, in light of Bryant's pain?

Touching his arm again, she smiled up at him. "Come on. Let's go look at maps."

She kept them in a drawer behind the gun-and-camera counter and showed them to customers on request only. Approximately 2-by-2½ feet square, geological survey maps covered an area of about twelve square miles, with all the elevations clearly marked. Pulling a mountain guide from a display rack, she turned to a fairly easy trail, then found a corresponding map.

When she spread the map out on the counter, Bryant shook his head at it. "This looks more complex than an anatomy chart."

The comparison made her laugh. "It's not, I promise you. And for this hike you don't need a compass. Look."

For the next twenty minutes she showed him how to find the trailhead and how to recognize notations on the map that corresponded with the descriptions in the book. Bryant had just started to feel confident with the map, when the twins and Matt burst through the door.

Seeing Deborah and Bryant, Ann and Lane came straight across to them. Matt hesitated only a second before starting toward the back of the store. When Bryant called him back, his chin jutted out and his eyes turned hard, but he came.

"What?"

"Deborah just showed me a good hike we could take this weekend."

"With you? I'm sure."

With a tip of her head, Deborah motioned for the girls to slip away. They didn't seem to need any encouragement. Exchanging looks, they backed away to put their book bags in her office. Perhaps if she hadn't just learned Bryant's story, she would have followed them. Instead, she flipped to a different page in the mountain guide.

"Or here's another one you might enjoy. It's not quite as long, and it goes to an overlook with a fantastic view. Although it has at least one really steep section, and parts of it might still be snowed over."

"I'm not sure I'm ready for a snowed-over trail yet," Bryant said. "The first one may be the best. What do you think, Matt?"

"You know what I think."

Bryant turned sideways to rest his hip against the counter and face his son. "I think you could give me a chance."

"Why don't you just shove it?"

Deborah winced. She couldn't imagine either of her daughters talking to her that way. And she knew it must be tearing Bryant apart inside. But he merely laid his hand on Matt's shoulder as though Matt hadn't spoken. "We'll buy you a good pair of boots."

Matt swatted Bryant's touch away. "Look. I hate this idea. Totally. The last person I'd want to go hiking with is you." With a wave of his arm, he swept both map and book onto the floor. "You don't have a clue about these mountains, and books won't help. I've been talking to kids at school. If I ever go, it'll be with someone who knows how. Like Deborah." Swinging his book bag over his shoulder like a club, he pivoted and stomped off through the store.

Bryant pressed his eyes closed and slumped against the counter. Despair radiated from him like heat. Impulsively, Deborah circled around and reached for his hand. "Don't give up. He'll come around."

His fingers tightened around hers. When he looked down at her, a lump formed in her throat. She wanted to take him in her arms and comfort him. She wished she could share the burden of his hurt.

No smile touched his lips and doubt filled his eyes. "Maybe he will. Probably he won't. But giving up isn't an option."

To lift his spirits a little, she laughed lightly. "Of course it's not. Besides, you're tougher than he is."

He glanced after his son, but of course Matt had disappeared. "His attitude seems as solid as rock, and I feel about as forceful as wet gauze."

Deborah doubled her hand into a fist and curled Bryant's hand around it. "Rock breaks scissors, paper wraps around rock. Do you remember that game?"

When he brought her hand up between them, pulling her closer, the mood of the moment changed suddenly. The noise and smells of the store disappeared and she was at Moose Flats again, by the stream, with the breeze teasing her hair and the water cascading down the rocks. Her tongue moistened her lips. Her breath caught in her throat.

When he spoke, his voice had lost its hard note of despair. "How do you do that? How do you make me hope again?" His free hand cupped her face. "How do you make me want?"

Want? It felt more like an ache, running hard and urgent from the base of her neck to the pit of her abdomen. He stirred feelings she hadn't experienced in thirteen years, he created needs she couldn't name. With her heart hammering against her ribs, she broke away. He'd promised her a year, then he would leave. Throwing her emotions his way would be like loading baggage on a train only to watch it leave without her. Swallowing hard, she struggled for control.

She stooped to pick the map and trail guide up off the floor, and her hands shook. It took two tries to roll the map so he could take it with him. When she thought she could speak calmly, she met his eyes again. "I think you should go ahead and buy this stuff. Sooner or later you'll get him to go with you."

He lifted his hand, then dropped it again. A muscle worked in his jaw. If he meant to comment on whatever had passed between them, he decided against it. "Sure."

"Don't forget your jeans and boots. You can have it all rung up at the same time."

"Tell Matt I'll be by to pick him up at the regular time."

"I could bring him home with me. We'd be a little later, but it would save you a trip."

"No. I don't want him to think he can scare me off."

Watching him leave, a bubble of tenderness burst inside her. Sooner or later he would win the heart of his son. He had too much love and strength of character to fail.

When Deborah didn't have a lot of things the kids could do, she kept them busy until five-thirty, then turned them loose to do homework if they had any. That way, they had money they could depend on, but she didn't have them idle on her payroll. About twenty minutes before she expected Bryant to come pick up his son, she realized she hadn't seen Matt for a while. Both twins were at her desk, talking more than studying, but Matt had disappeared.

After hearing Bryant's story of Matt's life, concern nipped at the back of her mind. Would he run away? With his history, could she rely on him to be like other teenagers she knew?

Keeping her concern to herself, she went to look for him.

He sat out on the loading dock with his legs hanging over the side. During the afternoon, a storm had started to move in, with overcast skies and a wind from the west. He looked incredibly alone in the gathering dusk, with his hair lifting and his shoulders hunched against the breeze. She caught back the sudden bite of tears. For his sake, as well as Bryant's, she wanted to help.

If he heard her approach, he didn't turn. When she got close enough to look over his shoulder, she saw why. In his ruled notebook, he'd sketched the line of mountains that Sterling nestled against. He'd caught their power, their majesty, and their menace. As though he'd lived here all his life, he saw them the way she did. Protecting, inspiring, but never to be trusted.

Awed, she sat down beside him. "Oh, Matt. How beautiful."

He whipped the notebook around to close it, but she flattened her palm against the page. "No. Please. Let me look at it some more."

"It's nothing."

"How can you say that? You're enormously talented."

"I can draw."

"No. You can feel. You make me feel."

Slowly, he opened the notebook again, and Deborah bent closer to trace a snow-filled bowl high on the north face of a higher peak with her finger. "The ice never melts there. Even in summer. Once my dad took a bunch of us up and we slid down it on plastic bags. Between the wind and the way the ice softens and refreezes over and over, it was so rough I came home covered with bruises.'' She pointed to an area of sheer granite cliffs. "A herd of bighorn sheep live here. My dad used to take trophy hunters up after them. We take photographers. You'd probably rather paint them.''

"I'd just like to see them.''

Intensity poured out of him, and he reminded her of Jay. Just thinking of it brought a smile to her lips. Jay had been fifteen when she fell in love with him. He'd been wild and reckless, but he'd loved the mountains the way she did. Under her father's tutelage they'd spent weekends and summers exploring and learning and getting tougher.

She remembered the exact moment she'd given Jay her heart. They'd found bear spoor, an adult and two cubs, and they'd followed it. They both knew the danger. An adult grizzly could tear a grown man to pieces; a female, protecting her young, charged at the slightest provocation. They found the bears fishing in a stream that ran high with winter melt. The mother scooped up a trout with her claws and tossed it to the cubs, who wrestled together over it. She caught another, then cuffed the larger cub into order before awarding it to him.

Silent as the trees, she and Jay had inched too close, then lain on their bellies and watched until the trio ate their fill and lumbered off. She could smell the dark scent of the female. She heard the heavy breathing of the cubs. She could almost feel the texture of their heavy spring coats. And when they left, her heightened senses transferred their awareness to Jay. When he pushed her over on her back, she'd opened her arms to him.

They'd never kissed before, but it felt as natural and right as the setting. They hadn't made love that day, but it didn't take sex to know she'd found her destiny.

She looked at Bryant's son and marveled at the twists of fate. He came from a background and up-bringing as far from Montana's mountains as possible, yet he knew their spirit and had the talent to put it on paper.

"Have you had much training?" she asked.

"A little. I got stuck in an art class here."

His choice of words brought a lump to her throat. Had he been hurt so much he had to protect every corner of his life?

"I thought the high school had a pretty good art teacher."

"She's okay. She wants me to enter something in the state competition."

"Are you going to?"

"It's pretty close to the deadline."

"So? Go for it." She tapped his sketch with her fingernail. "At least you won't embarrass yourself."

"Maybe." A sudden gust of wind ruffled the page, and Matt closed the notebook with a snap. "It's cold out here."

It was. The cold cement had numbed her bottom, and goose bumps covered her arms. Since sitting beside him, she hadn't once noticed. Now she hated to go back in, where defensiveness would again sharpen his voice and he would carry his anger like a shield.

Walking beside him, she could feel it building already. Before it took over, she decided to make an effort on Bryant's behalf. "Maybe if you went hiking with your dad Saturday, you'd find something that inspired you for the competition."

He stopped short and stared down at her. "You think I'd trust him? No way. Even if he knew anything about the mountains. *You* wanna teach me, fine. *He* can go to hell."

Stunned, torn, Deborah watched helplessly as Matt stomped away. Bryant faced this every hour of every day. He stared at it over the breakfast table and went to bed with it ringing in his ears. She remembered his determination to always be on hand for his son, and his willingness to take new risks in an effort to break down the barriers. She admired that kind of commitment. It made her feel emotions she hadn't experienced in years.

She followed Matt into the store, wondering if she should try to make him understand how much Bryant loved him. Maybe he would listen to her. Or maybe she would lose her tenuous rapport with him. And maybe Bryant would hate her for interfering, since he'd reacted so negatively to her previous efforts to help.

The background radio station had been changed from country to classic rock, which meant Lane had been fiddling with the dial. And above that, Ivy Hilgendorff's voice carried through the store. Someone had been testing perfumes in the personal-products aisle. Coming inside always felt like coming home. Jay had inherited the store from his father, and she had inherited it from Jay. It provided a good living for her and the twins, and gave her a base for the wilderness school.

But today she'd seen two sides of the same heartbreaking story, and she realized what a sense of permanence and belonging she'd been able to give her daughters because of this store. The three of them had shared years of happiness the Conovers would never know. And she had her own personal memories of love the way it should be.

Bryant had spoken of his former wife with agony in his voice, while she'd known nothing but good times with Jay. After all these years, she still treasured every day they'd had together.

She wished there were some way she could fill Bryant's heart with the inner peace she took for granted. Short of that, she'd have to settle for extending friendship and support to his son. At least she had a better sense of how to reach Matt. He had the mountain spirit, like Jay. Maybe Bryant did, too. Maybe, as Bryant hoped, that would be the key to breaking down the barriers.

Chapter Six

By the time they'd lived in Sterling three weeks, Bryant began to feel less like a fixture than he had at first. Most of his patients came for real medical reasons rather than to check him out.

He liked knowing not only his patients but their grandparents, their cousins, their next-door neighbors and their enemies. For the first time in his life he saw medicine as a social service as much as a profession.

On the other hand, he hadn't expected to be so lonely. He'd started to become acquainted with people, but he didn't feel part of the community. Deborah had done her best to introduce him around, but that didn't mean the locals took him to heart like some long lost brother. And this past week or so, Deborah had been too busy to give him much more than a nod when he went into the store.

He knew he should look on that as a benefit. The strong, immediate attraction that had driven him to kiss her at the stream still raced through him whenever he caught sight of her. A few minutes in her presence tended to dull his worry about Matt, and he couldn't afford to ease up on his efforts to save his son for even a second. But she was still the closest thing to a friend he'd found since coming to Sterling. He reminded himself he'd pay any price for Matt's sake, even loneliness.

But when the ring of the phone cut through the racket of Matt's stereo, Bryant grabbed for it eagerly.

"Bryant? It's Sara."

At the sound of his sister's voice, he settled into the couch with a smile. "Sara! How are you?"

"Oh, fine. My life is always the same. But I knew you wouldn't write. How are you doing? Is Matt making any progress?"

"We're adjusting. It's a big change."

"Everyone here's still convinced you're crazy. They're sure that since you weren't smart enough to put Matt in a rehabilitation center, he's going to end up in jail."

He ignored the flare of resentment at hearing what he already knew. "I love it when you're the bearer of good news."

Sara laughed. "It hasn't happened, has it?"

"Of course not. But there haven't been any miracles, either."

"He's a good boy."

Bryant leaned back and massaged the bridge of his nose. "If I didn't believe that, I wouldn't be here."

She laughed again. "Maybe I should fill you in on the latest gossip from home, to give you a break from cold reality."

That made him chuckle. Swinging around, he stretched out on the couch and propped his feet on the arm. "You haven't heard gossip until you've lived in a town this size."

"Probably not. But this has to be more interesting. We lost two maternity nurses—one got married, the other transferred to Metro General. Granddad added a new doctor to the staff in neurology, and Hal Martineaux's getting sued for malpractice."

"Hal's a good man. It's hard to believe he'd screw up."

Sara sighed. As an ob-gyn, she had to be on constant guard to avoid even the impression of negligence. "It's hard to believe any of us would."

"It's different here. Slower, less demanding."

"Do you like it?"

Her question surprised him, just because he'd found himself weighing the differences a lot lately. "I like being able to spend more time with patients. It seems natural to follow up personally." He chuckled. "I like the way people say thanks by dropping off a pie or a plate of brownies. I've even been asked to Sunday dinner once."

"I suggest you never hint at such heresy in Dad's hearing. Or Granddad's."

"You didn't ask me if I liked it best. It's just different here, that's all."

"Then I certainly won't ask. I know two senior doctors who are still very nervous about this experiment of yours."

"They know I'm coming back."

"Neither of them thinks you should have gone away."

"Stale news, Sara."

"Look, *I* think you made the right decision. Matt's got to be better off there. And as long as you're still at the top of the list for replacing Lindstrom, what difference does it make?"

Bryant closed his eyes and visualized the long beige hallways, the message bells, the smell of disinfectant. For the most part, he kept his own dreams buried beneath his mission to save Matt, but he ached for what he'd left behind. He wanted that position. Chief of family medicine. A goal so strong, held so long, didn't diminish in importance. Eleven months and his commitment would be finished here, and six months after that Jeffery Lindstrom would retire. He hoped that was enough time to accomplish a miracle.

As he approached Deborah's house, Bryant realized he'd lived next door to her for over a month and never been inside.

Ann opened the door, and the front room's lived-in hominess welcomed him. A wood-burning stove filled the fireplace opening and photographs of all sizes covered the mantel above it. An afghan had been thrown carelessly over the couch, a couple of magazines littered the floor in front of a wooden stereo cabinet and a coffee table under the side window held half a dozen houseplants. A huge orange cat slept in an old-fashioned wooden rocker. The television sat on top of an oak-veneer stand that looked as if it had come from a discount store, with a VCR on the lower shelf. Several videotapes lay haphazardly on the floor.

When Deborah came at Ann's call, Bryant decided she looked as tired as he felt. Too bad some things didn't wait until a convenient time. He got right to the point. "I'm supposed to come to you if I have a problem with my house, right?"

With a smile that didn't touch her eyes, she nodded. "What kind of problem?"

"My kitchen sink is leaking. When I got home today there was water all over the floor."

Fatigue colored her groan. As much as he needed his sink fixed, he wished he didn't have to bother her with it.

"Did you check to see where the leak was?"

"I think it's in the pipes underneath. I put a bucket under it."

This time her smile had more life. "If I were a plumber, you're the kind of customer I'd want. Let me get a couple of things, then we'll go take a look."

While he waited, Bryant looked at the photographs over the mantel. There were several of the twins, taken at various ages. There were group shots taken decades before, probably when Deborah was a child, and several newer ones of people he didn't recognize. Half tucked behind the rest, he found a professionally-taken picture of Deborah in a wedding dress, facing a young man. A very young man.

He lifted it off the mantel and turned it to catch the light at a better angle. He knew Deborah must have married early, to have daughters the twins' age, but her groom looked about seventeen or eighteen. Deborah looked radiant and in love. More in love than Nikki ever had been with him, even in the beginning.

"I'm ready," Deborah said from behind him.

Bryant turned to face her. "I hope you don't mind. You have quite a large extended family."

"We're pretty spread out." Setting a bucket filled with tools on the floor, she took the wedding picture and looked at it for a moment. Her eyes softened, the barest hint of a smile pulled at her lips, then she put it back behind the more current photos and picked up one of the group shots.

"This is my brother, Caleb, his wife, Tawnie, and their boys, Ryan and Todd. They live in West Yellowstone, where he works for the park service."

She handed it to him and picked up the next one. "Here's my sister, Rebecca, and her husband, Gary, with Eric, Lisa and Adam."

Interesting, he supposed, but only in relationship to her. Probably like most of her generation, both her brother and sister had moved away while she'd stayed. Why? What kept a woman with Deborah's drive and intelligence rooted in a town such as Sterling? When her husband had apparently died so young, wouldn't she have wanted to move on then?

She put both pictures back in place with a sigh. "Becca moved to Arizona about ten years ago, so I don't see her very often. She owns a boutique in Scottsdale, where she sells handmade craft decor. We'd better go get your sink fixed."

At the door she called over her shoulder. "Ann, try Judy's again. I want Lane to come home."

"Okay," Ann called back.

Bryant heard an edge in Deborah's voice, but couldn't tell if it was from worry or anger. Or fear. Vividly, he remembered her reaction to Nathan's fall on the boulder flow. When she pulled open the door, he hurried to hold it for her. "Am I interrupting something?"

Pausing to search his eyes, she weighed her answer. Suddenly he knew her concern didn't center solely on Lane. His stomach clenched, and he grabbed her arm.

"It's Matt, isn't it?"

Rather than pulling away, her hand came up to cover his. "It's probably nothing."

"If you know something, don't try to soften it. I went by the store to pick him up and Charlie said he hadn't seen him. Then I got sidetracked by the flood."

"He's with Lane. They went to Glen's to ride."

Her tone only made him more nervous. "What's the matter?"

"Ann said Matt's never been on a horse."

For all Bryant knew, Matt never had. "And?"

Deborah smiled, gave his hand a little squeeze and tipped her head toward his house. "Look, Lane's pretty levelheaded when it comes to animals, and they'll be home soon. Let's go fix your leak."

Unconvinced, Bryant followed across her yard and into his. He'd seen her shaky with concern over a minor head wound, but she ran two businesses too well to panic easily. Why did this situation worry her?

She didn't give him a chance to ask. When they reached his house, she went straight through to the kitchen and opened the cupboard under the sink.

The floor had dried, but water almost filled the bucket he'd put under the leak. Deborah knelt on the floor, stuck her head inside the cupboard and swore.

"Is it serious?"

"Not very. But it's a pain in the neck to fix. I'll have to turn your water off."

She wiped her palms on her jeans, took a flashlight from the bucket and headed for the cellar.

"Aren't you going to call a plumber?"

"In Sterling? Doctor, you crack me up." Poised at the top of the stairs, she laughed. It was the laugh he'd come to know, easy and open, the one that cleared away his clouds of worry like a benevolent summer wind. The one that made him want to touch her. Somehow she'd managed to bury her concern about Lane and Matt until no surface evidence remained. Did that mean no danger existed? Maybe he'd mistaken fear for annoyance. Maybe in his concern for Matt he'd read the wrong things into her reactions.

He took a deep breath and relaxed. He trusted her enough to accept her interpretation. If she refused to worry, so would he.

From the basement, he heard her footsteps on the concrete floor, the distant clanging of pipes, then she reappeared, coming up the stairs two at a time.

"Are you going to fix it yourself?" His incredulity must have sounded in his voice, because she laughed again.

"I told you it wasn't any big deal."

She crawled under the sink again, and he propped his hip against the counter. Had he once thought her like his mother? About as similar as a cockatoo is to a barnyard hen. And daily he discovered more reasons why he liked the hen very, very much.

"Is there anything I can do to help?"

"Hand me the pipe wrench?"

He looked at the assortment of tools in her bucket. "What's a pipe wrench?"

"Never mind." She reached out and hauled the bucket under the sink with her. Her legs stuck out into the room and her T-shirt had ridden up, leaving her middle bare. Trim. Smooth. Soft.

He imagined what it would feel like to run his hand over the curve of her hip. To unbuckle her belt. To unzip her jeans. Or to slide her shirt higher, past her ribs, over her breasts.

Heat spread through him and he pivoted away. Maybe if he hadn't kissed her that afternoon by the stream. Maybe if he'd never experienced her lithe body pressed against his. Then maybe he could think of her as the friendly neighborhood plumber.

Not in a million years.

She was warmth and hope. The most real person he'd ever met. And he wanted her.

With the precision of a scalpel, the truth cut deep. He'd wanted her yesterday and the day before. Ever since he'd kissed her. Perhaps from the moment he first caught sight of her swinging on a rope over the water.

The impossibility of it pressed down on him. Her close relationship with her daughters, the smallness of the town, the way her face softened when she looked at that photo of her husband. It all added up to a situation with stoplights flashing.

He had to make himself think of her as his neighbor, his landlord, his friend. Period.

She worked under his sink for about twenty minutes, and Bryant found himself comparing her to a surgeon, the way she knew what to do and proceeded through the steps without hesitation.

When the phone rang, he answered it, then held it out for her. "It's for you."

"Damn." She scooted out, which pushed her shirt so high on her midriff he had to look away. She wiped her cheek with the back of her hand, carefully curling her dirty fingers out of the way and still leaving a smudge.

He'd rarely seen anything so beautiful. So tempting. Forcing a friendly grin, he handed her a paper towel.

Her eyes connected with his, and the jolt hit him like lightning connecting with ground. Did she feel it? Or had he let his mind have too free a rein while watching her work?

She took the phone without touching his fingers.

Deborah forced her hand not to shake. With a look, a word, a touch, Bryant had managed to swamp her fear for Lane and Matt. Needs and drives she'd forgotten how to feel washed through her in waves. Unable to look at him and think at the same time, she put the phone to her ear and turned to face the wall.

"Hello."

"I got through to Judy," Ann said. "They're on their way home now."

"Good." They were in one piece. Lane had managed the horse. She could stop picturing one of them lying trampled in the pasture.

"If they come here first, should I send them over there?"

"Tell Lane to wait for me there. I won't be much longer." What she intended to say to Lane didn't need an audience.

"Okay. Sure."

"Thanks, honey."

Still not looking at Bryant, she hung up and headed for the sink. He blocked her before she could disappear under it again.

"Now that it's over, you might as well tell me."

It seemed silly, now. Lane had been working with horses all her life, and even though they didn't trust Nixon as a string horse, she knew how to handle him. Deborah leaned her hip against the counter and smiled to cover her embarrassment.

"Glen took most of the horses into the mountains with the current session. The only one left at his place is feisty. I was afraid Matt wouldn't be able to handle him. If they'd asked me, I wouldn't have let them ride him."

Without warning, Bryant cupped her cheek and rubbed at the smudge with his thumb. "No, I'm sure you wouldn't."

To her own surprise, Deborah didn't twist away. She liked his touch, the way his hand settled gently on her face, the way it sent heat radiating through her body. When he moved his hand down her throat, her pulse quickened under his fingers.

"What is it about you? Why do my troubles seem to disappear when I'm with you?"

"Don't." But her tongue flicked across her suddenly dry lips.

"I have to."

Moving closer, his mouth touched hers, gentle as a breeze. Then he pulled her against him and urgency took over. When her body turned liquid, she grasped his upper arms for steadiness. Old emotions mixed with new ones. Responses she barely remembered multiplied into a spectrum of needs that transcended thought. She slid her hands to his shoulders, his neck, into his hair, pulling him closer still and pushing back the limits.

His tongue teased her lower lip and she met it with her own. His hands cupped her bottom and lifted her against him. She welcomed the contact and held him tighter. The room dissolved around her. Time evaporated. She let the sensations of the moment envelop her.

The screen door slammed. Like a rifle report, it echoed through the room, followed by a deadly silence.

Shaken, guilty, disoriented, Deborah broke free of Bryant's arms.

Matt stood just inside the kitchen with betrayal etched on his face. Lane's shock quickly changed to a grin.

"Way to go, Mom." She nudged Matt in the ribs with her elbow. "We leave them alone for an hour, and look what happens."

Matt looked as if he'd been turned to stone. Horror filled Bryant's eyes.

Lane didn't notice. "Ann said you were worried, but everything went great. Nixon let Matt and me ride him double. I got on first and went around the pasture a few times, then Matt got on and I led him around a little bit. Then Nixon just stood there, gentle as you please while I got on, too. I think Matt's a natural. It was great."

"I'm glad you didn't break your neck. Look, will you go peel some potatoes for supper? I have to finish up here."

Lane laughed, and the sound swirled incongruously through the tension between Bryant and Matt. Deborah wanted to escape with Lane. For two cents, she'd leave Bryant and his son and his pipes and never come back. But if she did, he might not figure out how to get his water turned back on.

"As long as it's the *plumbing* you need to finish." Lane touched Matt's arm briefly and backed out the door. "See you tomorrow, okay?"

He didn't answer. He kept staring at Bryant with bitter eyes, while Bryant's search for the right words played across his face. When Matt sprinted suddenly toward the living room, Bryant grabbed for his arm. Matt swore and jumped out of reach.

Nausea rose in Deborah's throat. She'd seen edges of the problems between Bryant and Matt, but now she looked into the core. Even as Matt's footsteps pounded up the stairs, his animosity hung heavy in the kitchen.

Because of her. Because Matt had caught her kissing Bryant. Sick and trembling, she dived under the sink to finish the job and go home.

Far into the night, Deborah lay staring at the dark ceiling and reliving the scene in Bryant's kitchen. The kiss. Matt's tantrum. The kiss. The tantrum. Until the two events blended into one.

She'd lost herself completely in that kiss. If she'd been lifted out of her own life and thrust into another dimension, it couldn't have seemed more disconnected from the world she knew.

For twenty years she'd held Jay's love in her heart, and not once in all that time had she found another man attractive, let alone looked at one with desire. Sometimes, when she looked at a picture of him, she realized many of her memories of him had faded, but her love for him had stayed true.

Suddenly, Bryant Conover had changed everything. He made her feel, and want, and need. He brought strange hungers to life.

And the last thing he needed was a flirtation with her.

Matt's angry face filled her mind. And Bryant's hurt. They needed to concentrate on each other. They needed time and togetherness. They didn't need outsiders complicating things. She could probably help them most by staying away from Bryant.

She closed her eyes and tried to think of Jay. But no matter how hard she tried, the face that filled her mind belonged to Bryant.

Bryant closed the door of the first examination room only to have Shirley thrust another patient card in his hand.

How many of these had he seen today? Five? Fifteen? It felt like a hundred. Since Matt had walked in on him and Deborah the night before, he hadn't slept, he hadn't been able to eat. His relationship with his son was worse than it had ever been in Milwaukee. So much for dreams of conciliation.

Matt acted as if Bryant had committed murder. As if kissing Deborah were a personal betrayal.

Bryant wished he could put it out of his mind, but none of the patients he'd treated today had complaints major enough to require much concentration. He looked at the card in his hand. This one didn't hold much more promise than any of the rest.

Inside the second examination room were a young mother and her daughter. He checked the form. Name: Kimberlee Alldredge. Age: Six. Symptoms: Chronic fatigue. She sat on her mother's lap, with her head resting on her mother's shoulder. Her eyes were dull, her skin pale.

Bryant smiled at the mother. "Mrs. Alldredge? I'm Bryant Conover." He pulled his stool close and sat on it to be at eye level with the child. "And you must be Kimberlee."

Kimberlee smiled and nodded. Her two upper front teeth were just coming in and looked too big next to their tiny baby neighbors.

"How do you feel?"

"Tired."

With Tricia Alldredge, he reviewed Kimberlee's symptoms, then gave her a quick physical. Possible anemia. A blood test would indicate the extent. He asked about the family's history, which helped slightly. Tricia's hematocrit had been low during both of her pregnancies and iron supplements hadn't seemed to help.

He spent ten unhurried minutes talking with Tricia and getting to know Kimberlee, then he sent Shirley in to prick the girl's finger for a blood sample.

Following old habits, he went back to the first examining room. When he found it empty, he checked the appointment book on Shirley's desk and found he had half an hour before his next appointment. Half an hour to think and brood and worry.

Any other day he'd be appreciating the break. After a month in Sterling, he'd discovered he liked being able to take extra time with a patient without feeling pressured. Today, his problems with Matt weighed down on him.

The boy wouldn't talk, refused to listen, rejected every effort Bryant made to explain or reason. His anger raised his sulking to new heights—or new lows, depending on your point of view.

Pouring himself a cup of coffee, Bryant took it to his office and pulled some medical texts off the shelf to start exploring possibilities.

About the time his coffee got too cool to finish, Shirley brought him the results of the girl's blood test. From her expression he could tell the news wasn't good. Silently, he took the paper and checked the figures. A twenty-count hematocrit, when thirty-eight to forty was normal.

Suddenly his preoccupation with his personal problems shifted to other concerns. He cursed Sterling's isolation. He wanted technicians and testing facilities and second opinions.

"Take another sample," he instructed. "Let's run a white-cell count. I'll tell Mrs. Alldredge we'd like to see Kimberlee again in three or four days."

There were several things it could be, and at least one of those possibilities meant heartache for the family. He pulled a couple of medical texts off the shelf to see how many he could eliminate with the little data he had at hand.

Before he'd scanned the first entry, Shirley poked her head back into the room. "It's Irwin Freed. You know, with the county sheriff? He has Matt with him."

It took Bryant a second to reorient himself, then reality came smashing back. Matt had screwed up again, and after last night Bryant should have seen it coming.

"Send them in."

Bryant knew Sterling didn't have much of a police force; just two county deputies to insure people didn't break the speed limit and to answer minor complaints. He'd met Freed a couple of times but didn't know him. Now gratitude toward the man flowered inside him. Freed guided Matt with a hand on his arm and hadn't restrained him in any way.

"Hate to be the one to tell you we caught your boy here speeding out on the highway in a stolen car."

Numbly, Bryant rested his hip against the corner of his desk. The hell of the past few months suddenly paled compared to this. In Milwaukee there had been shoplifting and some minor vandalism. Even a little truancy. Never a hint of anything as extreme as grand theft. He searched Matt's face, but his son's eyes were blank and cold. "I thought you were in school."

"Too bad he wasn't," Irwin said. "Look, I called over to the county seat on the radio. Because it's a first offense and there was no property damage, we're going to leave him here with you, but you'll have to keep an eye on him. You'll be notified about when he'll have to go see the judge."

Relief roared through Bryant's head like a tornado. *A warning.* For stealing a car. Back home, it might have taken every marker his family could call in to rescue Matt from such a scrape.

Then the full impact hit. How could he stop Matt from doing it again? Or trying something worse? What changes could he make that would help? He swallowed his fear and offered his hand to Irwin. "Thank you."

A few more words, a few more seconds to let the cold fill his body, then Irwin left and Bryant faced his son alone.

Matt's expression grew more hostile as soon as the door closed, and Bryant half wished they had put Matt in jail. Maybe the threat of the law would have an impact.

"Why, Matt?"

Shooting a scathing look at Bryant, Matt turned toward the window. "Go to hell."

"Were you on anything?"

Matt glared straight ahead.

"Answer me. Were you on anything?"

With a snort, Matt shook his head. "That's what you'd like to think, isn't it? That drugs made me do it."

"Then why? Because I kissed Deborah?"

"What do you care?"

"I'm your father."

"What the hell difference does that make? What the hell difference has it ever made?"

Bryant battled despair, refusing to believe it was too late. "I love you, Matt."

"Right."

Longing to touch his son, to hold him and soothe away the hurt, Bryant plunged his hands into his pockets. "I never deserted you. For fifteen years I've wanted the chance to be your father. But if you won't believe that, nothing I can say will change your mind."

"Say? I can tell by the way you act. If you cared, you'd consider what *I* want. You never ask me. You're just like everyone else. Nobody gives a damn about me."

"I can't answer for your mother, but I didn't have to take you in. I chose to."

"That's why you dragged me away from my friends, to live in this godforsaken hick town."

"We've been over this before. When you started messing around with drugs, you gave up your right to make your own decisions. The alternative would have been a hospital.''

"So you say!"

Bryant reached out. "Matt—"

Matt jerked away. "Just leave me alone."

"Even if I wanted to, I couldn't do that. I'm your father, and you're my responsibility."

"You mean *liability*. If I weren't around, you could sleep with her any time you pleased."

Bryant grabbed Matt's shoulders. They were almost the same size, and their eyes met levelly. But in Matt's he saw the hurt. Hurt so deep it made him want to cry.

"Nothing is more important to me than you. I put my career on the line to come here, in an effort to give us a chance. You and me. Together. *No one* is more important to me than you. I would never let Deborah come between us—or anyone else. Do you understand?"

Matt jerked away to stand with his face to the wall. Although he obviously tried, he couldn't quite keep his shoulders from shuddering. Bryant ached for the agony inside his son.

"I wish I was dead," Matt said.

Chapter Seven

Deborah heard about Matt within minutes of his arrest. Ivy Hilgendorff saw Irwin haul Matt into Bryant's office and headed straight for the Merc, no doubt spreading the news along the way.

A tight knot formed in Deborah's stomach as she listened to a recital of how Irwin held Matt's arm in a grip of steel and how Matt had the very devil in his eyes. Of course, Ivy didn't know *exactly* what the problem was, but she continued to rattle on and on until Deborah wanted to scream. When Sam O'Roark came in, Deborah actually pointed him out to Ivy, who scurried right over to be the first with the news. It made Deborah an accessory to gossip, but she didn't care. She wanted a chance to think about Matt, and Bryant, and to determine if there was anything she could do.

First of all, she needed to get the facts. Knowing it would only excite more talk to be concerned, she called Shirley.

"This is Deborah. I heard Irwin picked Matt up. Do you know anything about it?"

Shirley hesitated just a second, then lowered her voice to a whisper, which let Deborah know she'd gathered her information by eavesdropping. "He stole a car. I don't know whose. He skipped school and took off. Makes your heart just bleed for poor Dr. Conover. I mean, the look on that boy's face was mean as a caged bear's. After Irwin left he started yelling at the doctor and swearing. Words you wouldn't believe."

Deborah's knees buckled and she sank into the chair behind her desk. She could hear Matt's voice and imagine Bryant's hurt. "Oh, Lord."

She let Shirley talk a little more before hanging up. As surely as she knew her own name, she knew what had precipitated Matt's actions. Kissing Bryant yesterday. She'd seen Matt's reaction. She'd felt his anger. Because of their indiscretion, he had made a mistake that might haunt him for the rest of his life.

When Bryant came into the store that afternoon, Deborah curbed the impulse to rush over to him. She wanted to. From her heart to her hands, she wanted to offer him comfort and reassurance. But reaching out to him could only lead to more trouble, so she stayed at the checkout stand.

He met her eyes, and the expression in his frayed her resolution. How could she maintain a distance from him, if one look sent her heart pounding? How could she keep her emotions in check, when he looked as if he'd tangled with a mountain lion? He drifted over to the magazine rack, obviously to wait for her, and she paged Charlie to come up front and cover the till.

Up close, Bryant looked so defeated Deborah's heart twisted in her chest.

"I need to talk to you."

She hoped he'd come to the same conclusions she'd reached. They couldn't let whatever had flared between them hurt Matt again. "Of course. Let's go out back."

But once the warehouse doors swung closed behind them, he pulled her against him. She hesitated only a moment before wrapping her arms around his waist. Comfort first, then reality.

"How's Matt?"

Bryant exhaled harshly, and his breath stirred her hair. "Angry. Hurt. Frustrated. Belligerent. Scared. Take your pick. The school agreed to take him back. Reluctantly, on probation. He's in my office doing homework, so I can't stay long."

"What are you going to do?"

"Hang on, I guess. I hoped there would be some progress by now. Coming here was supposed to bring us closer together."

"A month isn't very long."

"It passed so quickly, I'm afraid the year will be up before we solve anything."

Gently, Deborah pushed free of his embrace. It felt too right, discussing Matt like concerned parents. But Matt wouldn't welcome her involvement. Worse, if she let herself care too much, when Bryant eventually returned to Milwaukee, the loss could break her heart.

"What are you going to do?"

"I don't know. God, I wish I did." He paced a few strides away, then pivoted back. "How do I make up for what he sees as a lifetime of rejection? How do I convince him I'm on his side?''

"Keep loving him."

"He refuses to believe I do. He misinterprets everything."

"One of these days he'll let down his guard, and you'll be there."

Jamming his hands in his pockets, Bryant shook his head. "I'm tired of waiting. But when I try to take action, he shuts me out. How do I get past that? You have experience with teenagers. Give me some answers."

She wished she could, but she'd never been faced with a challenge like this. By comparison, her life with the twins had been a dream.

Before she could say anything, Lane pushed through the swinging doors and Deborah sucked in a little breath. Seconds sooner, and Lane would have caught her in Bryant's arms again. Yesterday's interruption might have gone down fine; today didn't need any more complications.

"Umm, look," Lane began, then hesitated.

"Come on in, sweetie. You're not interrupting anything."

"Well, I just wanted to say, about Matt . . ."

Bryant tensed. "If you know anything that will help, tell me."

Sensing her daughter's uncertainty, Deborah laid her hand on Bryant's arm. "Only if you won't be breaking a confidence."

"It's not that. I just think if Matt spent a session with Lodestone it would really help him. He wants to, he talks about it all the time, but I don't think he'd come right out and ask."

Bryant laughed harshly. "When I wanted to take him hiking, he refused."

Deborah remembered how Matt had scorned Bryant mostly for his lack of skill and experience. She remembered the affinity for the mountains she'd seen in his sketches. In light of both, Lane's proposal seemed both simple and appropriate. "This is different," she said. "It might make a difference."

"There's only two more weeks of school," Lane pressed. "He might not be so restless if he had that to look forward to."

A muscle knotted in Bryant's jaw. "Whoa, Lane. I know you want to help, and I'm sure Matt's hinted broadly about going. But—"

Deborah cut in before he got too entrenched in his rejection of the idea. "Let me talk it over with Bryant, okay? Thanks for bringing it up."

"Well, I just thought if it would help..."

"It might be the answer, honey. But there are a lot of things to consider. Now, how about if you hustle back to work?"

"Sure." Lane shot a penetrating look at Bryant before swinging away.

Bryant picked up his objections where he'd left off. "Your wilderness program isn't slanted for kids with problems, and Matt doesn't have the faintest idea what he'd be getting into. What if he rebelled when it got rough? You haven't seen him at his worst. It could spoil the trip for everyone else."

Deborah thought the challenge would do Matt good, not to mention how much he'd benefit from such a total change of environment. Better still, why shouldn't they both go? Bryant already saw the challenge of the mountains as a way to bridge the gap with

Matt. Going with an organized group might make it sit better with Matt, while giving Bryant the opportunity he needed. Glen was taking the session scheduled for the week after school got out, and if she remembered correctly they still had a couple of spaces available.

"I think you should let him go, Bryant. Lodestone may not be a specialized leadership school, but challenging the mountains changes people."

"You can't guarantee it would change him to be more accepting of me."

Mentally crossing her fingers, she took a deep breath. "It might if you came, too."

The suggestion took Bryant by surprise. She saw it hit, watched him fight the idea, saw it evolve from absurd to reasonable in his mind, then watched doubt surge again.

"Don't worry about your practice. Everyone knows you have to take a vacation sometime. We could get along for ten days."

"But—"

"It's what you've wanted, to get away together with Matt, only this time he can't argue that you don't know what you're doing, because you'll be with the school."

Bryant stared out the open loading door at the mountains to the east. The muscle worked in his jaw and he exhaled deeply before turning back to her.

"On one condition. That you make sure we get in a group *you're* leading. Matt thinks you're the foremost expert."

No! Her mind screamed the answer. Ten days at close quarters. Ten days with Matt watching over their shoulders. This very minute she wanted to touch

Bryant, hold him, feel his lips on hers again. It would be much better if he and Matt went with Glen.

Every reasonable argument weighed the scale in favor of staying as far away from him as possible. For Matt's sake, and for her own. But how could she turn Bryant down when he looked at her like that? How could she resist when she reacted to him in ways that had nothing to do with logic?

When Shirley handed Bryant the results of Kimberlee Alldredge's blood test, he accepted them with grim determination.

The days since Matt's arrest had been hell. He'd been on edge. Matt had stayed surly. Communications had ground to an absolute halt. He'd welcome anything that would take his mind off his problems.

He opened the folder and scanned the figures and relief poured through him. Normal white-cell count. Not leukemia. Thank God.

With the worst possibility out of the way, he pulled some medical texts off the shelf and began comparing what he already knew with what he wasn't sure of. Listing the strongest possibilities on a yellow pad, he realized he had no family medical history. Not only did he have no records to turn to, he had no idea who the previous doctor was—or if they even had one.

Bozeman was far enough away that people from Sterling didn't bother with medical care except for emergencies. Kimberlee's problem certainly warranted treatment, but when would Tricia Alldredge have decided her condition was serious enough to make the trip?

The question reminded him of Deborah's assertions that these people deserved medical care as much as anyone else. And of course they did. But there were so many other factors. He could afford to work here for a year because he had a good financial portfolio. But a practice like this would never draw a new doctor straight from school with debt up to his eyebrows and high expectations.

As in any business, people got what they paid for. If rural America couldn't pay for a doctor, what more could they expect? But then, what happened to people such as Kimberlee Alldredge? He was pretty sure she had a rare blood disease called spherocytosis, something he'd seen only once before. What would she do without care? How long could she go without diagnosis? It was rarely fatal, but caused severe anemia and needed to be monitored. Sometimes it required a splenectomy. Wondering about it, Bryant suddenly felt indispensable.

Leaving his books and notes where they were, he went down the hall to check when he'd see Kimberlee next. As though she'd been in his office only that morning, he could see her in his mind's eyes, her pale face resting against her mother's shoulder.

How often had he walked into an examining room to find a mother and child in that exact position? Probably hundreds of times. How often had he had time to consider them as individuals? Rarely. Only when they were seriously ill, and in cases like that he referred them to specialists. Occasionally he found out later what happened, but too often they simply became some other doctor's patients.

For the first time, Bryant realized that at Conover Memorial he'd been a cog on a wheel. His appointments had been scheduled ten minutes apart, and if he took time to go to the bathroom or spent too long with someone, he got behind.

This rural practice gave him time to indulge in people and get to know them. Kimberlee, for instance. She depended on him. When more blood tests provided a positive diagnosis, he would consult with a hematologist, but she would stay his patient. A condition such as hers might require long-term monitoring, which meant her care and well-being would be up to him for a long time. Maybe years.

No. He wouldn't be in Sterling that long. He'd be returning to Milwaukee next spring—whether he succeeded or failed with Matt.

He suppressed a sigh. In the meantime, following up with Kimberlee would keep his mind occupied while he waited for summer. And Lodestone. And spending ten days with Matt in the mountains.

The sun hovered briefly on the rim of the mountains, turning the thin horizontal clouds to gold. As it dropped out of sight, the color changed to pink, then faded to aqua and gray. The breeze picked up, bringing with it a chill from the snow that remained at the higher elevations. Lodestone's fifteen participants zipped their jackets, turned their collars up and congregated eagerly around the evening fire.

Deborah took a place between Ann and Lane. Bryant and Matt sat together on the other side of the circle, with a good foot between them. Since that afternoon at the store when Bryant had agreed to try this, Deborah had managed to keep a reasonable distance from him.

Not that it seemed to make any difference to Matt. He had continued to work for her and slowly accepted her efforts to resume a friendship, but things were as bad as ever between him and his father. Deborah's confidence that doing this together would help them had almost faded away. Bryant, on the other hand, had stayed optimistic in the face of Matt's attitude.

This first day had gone well for everyone else. Gesturing for quiet, Deborah reminded herself she had an obligation to the whole group, not just to Bryant and his son. She smiled at the faces lit by the flickering fire.

"Welcome to Lodestone. I noticed this afternoon that some of you have previous camping experience." She gave her regular welcome speech, then started on the rules.

"I can't stress enough how important it is to never, never leave camp without a buddy. The Madison Range is as rugged and unpredictable as any in North America. If you were alone and got hurt, there's a possibility you'd never be found. Two people together greatly increase the chances of survival."

Those who had come with a friend exchanged glances, affirming for each other that they'd stick close through thick and thin. Those who had come on their own scanned the group, checking out the possibilities. She'd already decided to make sure Matt had to work with Bryant.

"Second, don't tempt fate. Avoid the impulse to go just a little further or stay out a little longer. Listen to your body and stop before you're tired. Watch the sky, study your maps. It's always better to err on the side of safety."

She covered the rest of the list, watching for reactions that would help her understand her group better. By the time she finished she'd calmed most fears and inspired a good dose of enthusiasm. Whatever happened between Bryant and Matt, this would be a good session.

"Okay, that does it for tonight." She spread a generous smile at the group. "Get a good night's sleep. Tomorrow will be a busy day."

Bryant lay in his tent, listening to his son's even breathing mix with the noises of the night and thinking of Deborah.

Watching the way Matt responded to her all day, Bryant couldn't decide if he respected her or resented her. She'd developed a friendship with Matt, and although Matt definitely needed friends, Bryant couldn't help feeling jealous.

Worse, he had to hold his own feelings about her in check for fear of setting Matt off again. The ten days of this session looked like ten days of torture.

He shifted in his sleeping bag in an effort to get comfortable, and a couple of rocks rose out of the ground to form new lumps under his back. He had a high-density pad under his sleeping bag, the kind Deborah had recommended. She'd assured him he'd be as comfortable as in a real bed. He'd like to test her bed and see what she used as a frame of reference.

He had too much on his mind to sleep, anyway. He pushed free of the sleeping bag and pulled his sweatshirt on over his thermal underwear. As if it were midwinter, he put on jeans, hiking boots, mountain parka, watch cap. Unzipping the tent, he crept out into the night.

There was no moon, but light from a million stars filtered through the trees, outlining the shadowy forms of the two tents closest to his. The wind soughed through the trees and a few hushed voices still murmured from neighboring tents, but so quietly they sounded as natural as the creaking pines. Not far from the campsite, a stream rushed down the mountain, and Bryant imagined he could hear the cold of melting snow in its melody.

A twig snapped, startling him. He swung toward the sound, but it took a moment to spot the form coming his way. It took a moment longer to recognize it.

"Deborah?" He whispered her name, not wanting to disturb the stillness.

She drifted silently, like a shadow. "What are you doing up? Tomorrow's going to be a big day."

"I could ask you the same question. What are you doing prowling around?"

"Making sure everything is all right. I like to check out the camp before I go to bed, just to be sure."

"Sure of what? Bears?" Sudden apprehension raced through him. She was too small and fragile to face dangers alone.

"Of course not. There's just a certain feel to a secure camp. I sleep better if I reassure myself."

He'd sleep better if he knew *she* were safe in *her* tent. "Why don't you have a flashlight?"

"I have one in my jacket pocket."

"Oh, good. That makes me feel so much better."

Her soft laughter rippled into the night. "When there are no clouds, I can see better without one. Flashlights screw up your night vision. Want to come with me?"

"Without a light?"

"Sure. I'll even walk you home when we're finished."

For more reasons than lack of light, he hesitated. Since Matt's arrest, they'd maintained a distance from each other. They hadn't discussed the need for it, it had just happened. That didn't mean his attraction to her had evaporated.

If she happened to wear her hair loose, he wanted to sift his fingers through it. If he caught sight of her from the back, he wanted to come up behind her and wrap his arms around her waist. When she looked up at him with her blue eyes as clear as the sky, his mouth went dry with wanting.

For the first time in over fifteen years, a woman affected him as if he were a hot-blooded teenager. Since they both hoped this session would work miracles with Matt, he should pop back into his own tent and shut his mind to the image of her walking around alone. Midnight trysts could only make things more difficult.

Ignoring reason, he took her hand. "How can I turn down an offer like that?"

She laughed again, making his throat go dry, and led him toward the stream. He sensed that she went slowly out of consideration for him, that on her own she could move as surely as a deer. She was only a shape in the dark, small and familiar. Her loose hair fell over her shoulders and glistened in the starlight.

They passed the first tent, its dome a light blur against the shadows. "Those two guys from Washington," she whispered.

Bryant hadn't sorted people out enough to know which two guys she meant, but it didn't surprise him she knew who slept where. They circled the tent and moved on.

With each stride, Deborah grew more seductive to Bryant. Her assurance flowed through their linked hands to him. He knew dozens of competent women among the nurses and doctors and technicians at the hospital. None had opened his mind to the possibilities of a relationship.

Deborah made him crazier with longing here among the silent trees than any woman he'd ever known. Wanting more, he gripped her hand tighter.

They passed three more tents, and when they reached a place far enough from where people slept that they wouldn't be heard, he pulled her against him. Her breath brushed his cheek, then her hair, cold and silky, touched his chin. The fabric of her jacket rustled under his hands.

"Bryant, no."

"Don't argue." Lifting her chin, his lips found hers. The chill left by the air lasted only a second, then heat fused them together. How long since he'd kissed her? Weeks. A lifetime. She fit perfectly within his arms, the right size and shape to fill the emptiness of decades. She smelled of sun and wind, she tasted like adventure. The urge to explore every twist and turn into the unknown swelled inside him.

But the night was cold, the breeze brisk, and sanity still held on by its toenails. He lifted his head, while continuing to hold her close. "Are you finished with your inspection? Perhaps I should see you back to your tent."

Her laughter curled softly around them, tempting him to bury rational thought. She rose to press a quick kiss on his lips. "How chivalrous of you. Then how would you find your own?"

"You're not making this any easier."

With both hands, she cupped his face. "You're a good man, Bryant Conover. And someday Matt will recognize how lucky he is to have you for a father."

Her optimism only made breaking apart harder. Her kiss told him clearer than words that she wanted as much as he did, yet she could put Matt first. She was an incredible woman. And if he didn't know better, he might think he was falling in love with her—but that was impossible. Wasn't it?

Halfway through the session, Deborah taught the group about pack trips. After discussing what kinds of foods traveled well, they tried a few meals made with light, portable items. Then came lessons on how to pack both backpacks and horses. The finale of the session would be a four-day trip higher into the mountains.

Before that, they'd spend two days on orienteering, which meant map reading and compasses and working with a partner. Bryant and Matt had worked together all week without a break in the tension, making Deborah wonder if they'd all misjudged the depth of Matt's problems. When she sent them off on the second day to solve the riddle of the map, she did it with her fingers crossed.

They were the third team to be dropped off. Bryant knew Deborah had left no stone unturned in preparing them for this, but that didn't make him necessarily optimistic. They wore long pants, hiking boots, jackets and hats. Their day packs contained food and a first-aid kit, and they both had canteens strapped to their belts. They had a sheet of paper with instructions written in the strange notations of orienteering, a U.S. geological-survey map, a compass and a specific goal: to get back to the base camp by sundown. And Matt had spoken in nothing but monosyllables all morning.

After the truck droned out of earshot, the earth seemed absolutely still. Then a breeze Bryant couldn't feel whispered through the trees. A bird called from off to his left, and from the right another answered. The track where he and Matt stood was hardly visible, two ruts for tires, overgrown with grass crushed by the recent passing of the pickup. Between here and camp there was no trail. He'd have to rely on his own devices for the next seven to ten hours. And on the skills of his son.

But of all the members of the session, Bryant believed he had the best partner.

Matt spread the map open on the trunk of a fallen tree, and Bryant looked over his shoulder. There were two X's marked in red. Their starting point and their finishing point, which was the camp.

"We're only about three miles away, if we could go straight." Matt drew his finger in a line between the two marks, then backed it up and stopped it at a point in between. "And it's only about a six-hundred-foot descent, but this pcak's in the way."

The lines that marked changes in elevation indicated steep terrain under Matt's finger. They were to use the map, follow the directions on their instruction sheet, find the route that would be both direct and safe, and not get lost. Deborah or one of her assistants would check on each team at some point during the day.

Bryant crossed to the ridge of the hill. "That way?"

Matt checked the map, read his compass, looked at the sky and the position of the sun. "Yeah."

As the morning progressed, the extent of conversation between them consisted of deciding which way to go. A couple of times, when the terrain allowed, Bryant tried to draw Matt out. When that didn't work, he started asking more questions about their route, about how to read the map and use the compass, about what kind of time they were making. At least he could get several sentences in a row out of his son that way. And when they were dealing with the task at hand, Matt seemed like a different person. He had become the person who got along well with all the other members of the session. He was a boy with superior skills and likable qualities. A son a man could be proud of. For Bryant, it was a new and heady experience.

A little before noon they stopped to eat lunch. They'd been following a ridge of rock just above the tree line. The air was hot and dry and still. High overhead a pair of hawks circled on the currents of air, dipping occasionally, then rising again.

After gathering up every bit of paper and scrap of food they'd dropped during lunch, Matt spread the map again. Bryant leaned back against a rock and watched his son make decisions. Five months ago, nothing on earth would have prompted him to believe Matt could be this competent. Today, he'd willingly put his life in Matt's hands.

"We're supposed to hit this little valley," Matt said. "I think the ridge we're on tapers off a quarter of a mile from here. If we follow it, we'll end up in the right place."

Bryant studied the map and considered his son's proposal. So far, Matt had done a superb job. Their route had been pleasant and sensible. "Sounds good to me."

The ridge had a two-dimensional slope. Ahead of them, it slanted at an easy five or six degrees. Sideways, it tapered about two degrees for several yards, then fell off abruptly. For hiking purposes, it was as good as a trail. And Matt had judged it correctly. The quarter of a mile took them half an hour to hike.

Then it stopped abruptly.

Between the time the map had been drawn and now, an avalanche had tumbled the side of the mountain away.

Bryant looked down the fall of rock and tangled brush and shuddered. Whole trees had been splintered like matchsticks. Branches and roots twisted together around boulders the size of buildings. "Looks like we have a problem."

Before the session, he would have expected Matt to tear up the map, throw the compass at a rock, curse the day, the situation and his father. But a new, competent, self-sufficient Matt had started to emerge. He spread the map out on the ground to study the possibilities. Bryant hunkered down beside him.

"It looks like we have a couple of choices," Matt said. "First, we could backtrack a mile or so and hope to find a way that would take us around the ridge completely. Or we could go back to where we ate lunch and try to cut up over the avalanche this way." He followed one of the fine curved lines with his finger. Then he sat back on his haunches and considered the way before them. "Or, we could pick our way over the rock."

Bryant tried to weigh which would be fastest against which would be safest. None of the alternatives looked appealing. "How long do you think it would take to go back up and over?"

"A couple of hours, maybe more."

"Going ahead seems pretty dangerous."

"It'd be like bouldering," Matt said. "Like at Lake Thompson."

"If you stretch your imagination." Bryant could see how that boulder flow had probably started out like this—a century or two ago. Time and the elements would have decayed the vegetation and left barren rock. Logically, only the dead and broken trees made this flow different from that one. But before he could further consider the options, Matt began folding up the map.

"Let's cross the avalanche," Matt said.

Suddenly there were new factors to weigh in: Matt's self-confidence, and the long-term effect of this experience on their relationship. Though the trip looked difficult, it didn't look impossible. Maybe much of Matt's new strength came from Bryant's willingness to trust him. If so, Bryant intended to reinforce it. "It'll be slow going," he said.

"We have time." Matt tucked the map in the pocket of his day pack. "Just follow me."

Bryant admired his son's decisiveness and smiled with satisfaction at the skill with which Matt had brought them this far.

It turned out to be much more difficult than the boulder flow at Lake Thompson. The angles of the rock jutted more abruptly. None of the surfaces had worn smooth, and the broken trees and tangled brush added a wicked element. Matt seemed more sure on his feet than he had been then, but Bryant hadn't gained an equal amount of new confidence. Frequently Matt got far enough ahead that he had to wait for Bryant to catch up.

They cut across the slope at an easy angle, to keep the descent reasonable. Bryant judged the total distance at about a hundred yards. On level ground, with a clear field, an NFL running back could make it in seconds. No such easy going here. Sometimes the ruin of trees blocked their way and they had to go back up and around. After more than an hour of careful progress, he guessed they'd made it about three-quarters of the way.

On a fairly clear angle, Bryant hit a loose rock. When it tilted slightly, he pulled back but he'd given it too much of his weight. It slipped and he went down. He flailed at a broken tree limb and tore a gash in his arm. The rock tumbled out from under him and he slid into a shallow crevice of rock, landing hard on his hip.

He must have cried out when he went down, because Matt's voice echoed back immediately.

"Dad! *Dad!*"

Pain surged through Bryant's foot and leg. He swallowed it, shaking his head against the fog that threatened to pull him under. "Here, Matt. Over here."

Fighting nausea, he tried to pry himself out of the wedge of rock and find a surface smooth enough to sit on. The movement sent a new wave of pain screaming up his leg.

"Oh, Dad. Don't try to move yet. Just a sec. Oh, God."

Bryant couldn't follow what Matt did. Agony battered him again, then ebbed.

"I got your foot out, Dad. Here, put your arm around my shoulder. Watch it. Careful. There. Lean back. Okay. Here, have a drink."

"How bad is it?"

"I don't know. Bad. What should I do? Oh, God, it's all my fault."

Bryant took another drink of water. The pain had started to ease off, probably because Matt had managed to get his injured leg propped straight. With clarity came awareness of more than the accident. Matt was calling him *Dad*. Had called him Dad over and over. They could amputate his leg at the knee and he wouldn't miss it. This fall had gained him something he'd begun to doubt would ever be his.

"Slow down. Everything's going to be okay." He eased himself onto his elbows, waiting for a fresh onslaught of agony. It didn't come. Good.

With Matt crouched at his side, pressing a hand against the shin, his face a study in distress, Bryant touched his son's shoulder. "Hey, hang in there. Everything's going to be fine."

"Yeah. Sure. Look, Dad, we've got to stop the bleeding."

Slowly, Bryant's training began to surface. He tried to move his leg and instantly regretted it. "You're going to have to cut my pant leg, son, so we can see what we've got."

"It's already ripped."

"Okay, ease your hand off. Let me see what the blood flow's like."

Bryant had Matt wash the blood away with water from a canteen and expose the gash on his shin, then talked him through getting it taped shut. During that process he realized the contusion wasn't his worst injury.

He'd broken at least one of the bones near his ankle.

Chapter Eight

Seeing the avalanche from across the valley, Deborah wondered how Lodestone had managed to run classes all spring and into summer without discovering it. The swath of rock looked bright and raw in the late afternoon sun, and was too obvious to be missed. Clearly by varying their base camps to avoid overusing any one particular area, they hadn't picked this route before.

Had Bryant recognized the danger? If he and Matt decided to avoid it, which way would they go?

She nudged her horse forward, slicing diagonally down the hill, picking her way through the trees, from pine to aspen and then out into the open.

Once out of the trees, she uncased her binoculars for a better look. The gash of avalanche wiped out half a mountain's worth of vegetation. Magnification brought each rock and mangled tree into clear focus. She scanned the ridge first, the one Bryant and Matt would probably take. In the heat of the afternoon, she saw no movement at all. No deer or elk, no coyotes. No people. She didn't know whether to be relieved or nervous.

Starting where the avalanche tore across the ridge, she panned from side to side, gradually moving down the slope. A movement caught her attention, and suddenly Matt's back filled her field of vision. He leaned forward in an unnatural way, and behind him she saw Bryant. An old, old panic surged through her. Jay, broken and bleeding on the road. Bryant, sprawled on a dangerous pile of rock. She kicked the horse's flank and tightened her knees against his shoulders.

She tied the horse at the bottom of the flow, where the jagged boulders started massing on top of each other and several feet of packed ice still hadn't melted.

"Bryant!"

Matt whipped around, waving frantically. "It's my dad. Hurry."

Oh, please God, don't let it be bad. As quickly as possible, she clambered toward them.

She saw the blood first. Dark on the pale rock, glistening in the sun. Her stomach tightened painfully. But Bryant looked alert, even with the rough bandage on his shin still growing darker with blood. His ankle had been bound firmly, and his forearm had been wrapped with gauze. She wanted to grab him, to hold him, to reassure herself he was all right. Instead, she forced the panic from her face and knelt beside him.

"Are you okay?"

"Matt's a terrific first-aider." But his voice sounded weak and uneven. The strain of staying under control showed in his face.

Matt's face had paled beneath its tan and his hands still shook. "It's all my fault."

"Of course it's not." Bryant struggled onto one elbow and Deborah knelt to help him.

"I said to come this way," Matt persisted.

"We both decided."

"You agreed so I wouldn't throw a tantrum."

"I agreed because you've proven yourself over and over again this trip."

Matt opened his mouth, then shut it again. If the situation hadn't been so critical, Deborah might have laughed at the emotions playing across his face. He'd been so used to fighting, he didn't know how to accept Bryant's praise.

"You haven't made a single bad call since we set up camp," Bryant added.

"Except this one."

"Come here, son."

Time seemed to hang in the air while Matt stared at Bryant's upraised hand. When he came close enough to hunker down and clamp it, Deborah let out a breath and felt Bryant do the same.

"If anyone here is to blame, it's me. I'm older and have more experience, and I recognized that coming across the avalanche could be dangerous. But I didn't want to backtrack. I'm glad you can see how a different decision might have been better, but you didn't cause the accident. Nobody will ever hold this against you, especially not me."

"You're not mad?"

"Of course not."

Deborah felt the tightening of Bryant's grip around Matt's hand. She watched the acceptance that passed between them. She fought back tears of happiness for them both.

She had fallen in love with Bryant. Head-over-heels, stars-in-her-eyes, pure-and-simple, heart-stopping, in love. It hit her between the eyes with such intensity, her vision clouded and her lungs contracted.

She hadn't expected it. She wasn't prepared for it. And because she didn't know how to deal with it, she forced it aside. Physically, she'd been attracted to him from the beginning. But she'd loved once, long ago, and had never, ever expected to experience it again.

Especially for someone who didn't belong to her world.

When Bryant shifted to sit straighter, she moved to give him more support. "How bad's the ankle? Or is the gash the worst of it?"

"Something's broken. I haven't tried to stand on it, but it hurts like hell. The wound on my leg will have to be sutured."

"Do we need to airlift you out?" She forced a lightness she didn't feel into her voice. Having a doctor was supposed to eliminate the need for things like that.

"Not if you and Matt can help me down."

She estimated the distance between them and the horse. Probably fifteen yards, but as rough as any terrain could be. "Depends on how much you can help."

"I don't think there's anything wrong with the rest of my body."

She touched the bandage on his arm. "What about this?"

"A scratch."

Matt swallowed so hard she heard his gulp. "It'll need stitches, too."

Her heart swelled with pride in Matt. He'd done so well, performing like a mature, responsible person. And Bryant had never stopped believing in him. "Any shock?"

"A little. Not much."

"Okay. Let's try to get you upright."

It took all three of them. Deborah steadied Bryant's leg while Matt gave him his strength. Slowly Bryant levered himself up against the boulder. One rock at a time, they went over and around, discussing each move in advance, planning each shift in direction. After nearly an hour they hit flat dirt, and by then all three were hot, sweaty and tense.

Using Bryant's uninjured leg, Matt boosted him belly first onto the horse. Deborah knew it took everything Bryant had to pull himself on and twist to a sitting position. He looked so pale she was afraid he'd fall back off.

"We'll walk on either side of you," she told him. "Hold on, and if you think you're going to faint, say so."

He smiled, but she could tell it was forced. "Why couldn't you just build me one of those drag carriers the Indians used?"

"Because I'm not an Indian. Besides, we'd probably belong to a tribe that would leave you out here to die a noble death."

"Did Indians really do that?" Matt asked incredulously from his side of the horse.

Deborah laughed, since anything was better than thinking. "I haven't the faintest idea. After the effort it took to get your father this far, it just sounded like a good idea."

"Thanks," Bryant muttered.

"You're welcome." Later, when she could indulge her feelings, she'd decide how to deal with her new emotions for Bryant and his son. Until then, she had to get Bryant off the mountain and into Bozeman. Until then, maybe she could pretend nothing had changed.

Deborah parked in front of her mother's house and slumped back in the seat with her eyes closed. She couldn't remember when a wilderness session had left her so totally exhausted. Before, whenever she'd had to bring an injured participant down, she'd managed to go back and give the rest of the group their money's worth. This time she hadn't been able to get Bryant out of her mind.

The vision of him lying bruised and bloody on the rocks haunted her dreams. Awake, she kept wondering whether he and Matt had been able to build on what they'd started. The twins noticed how preoccupied she was, and her lax leadership had put a heavy burden on her two assistants the final four days of the session.

She hated being so unfocused. And so confused. And so tired. Somehow she had to pull herself together. Her life wouldn't go on hold just so she could puzzle things out. But she'd give a week's profits from the Merc for a day without commitments.

Heaving a sigh, she climbed out of the car and took the box of groceries from the trunk.

Naomi had a half-finished quilt set up in the living room, positioned so she could sew and watch television at the same time. Kissing her mother's cheek, Deborah exclaimed over how little there was left to do.

"Your hands haven't been giving you any trouble, I see."

Naomi flexed her fingers. "Actually, we'll probably have a storm by the end of the week."

Deborah went on through to the kitchen to put the groceries away and fill the kettle for tea. "How are you feeling generally?"

"Quite wonderful. I hadn't realized how much those monthly trips to Bozeman took out of me. I appreciate your doctor more than I thought I would. And he has such a marvelous way of dispensing advice. I find it much easier to follow doctor's orders."

Mention of Bryant sent warmth flowing from Deborah's heart to her toes, and raised her mental confusion another notch higher. Refusing to acknowledge either reaction, she shut the cupboard door with a snap.

When Naomi's arthritis forced her into a wheelchair, Deborah had talked her into making the kitchen more convenient. The counters were now low and cantilevered to permit sitting access. It meant Deborah had to bend over to use the stove and the sink, but Naomi had an amazing amount of self-sufficiency.

With the gas burning blue under the kettle, Deborah smiled and dropped into a straight-backed chair, hooking her heels on the rung. Naomi maneuvered her chair to the other side of the table with the skill of long practice.

"Did you finish the session without any more problems?"

Since the question didn't touch her emotional state, Deborah could answer truthfully. "Nothing out of the ordinary. Ann developed a crush on a *cool* law student who plans to save the planet.''

With a soft laugh, Naomi took two mugs from low-hanging hooks. "I can see both those girls leading you on a merry chase a couple of years from now.''

"We can always hope they fall for local boys.''

"Or we can be more realistic and expect them to move away when they grow up.''

At the suddenly serious note in Naomi's voice, Deborah met her eyes. "You know I'll do anything to keep them here.''

"No. You'll try to make it possible for them to stay. If you didn't understand the difference, you wouldn't work so hard.''

The kettle whistled, and Deborah poured water over bags of lemon tea. Sitting back down, she cupped her mug between both hands with a little sigh. "Can I win this battle? Can I keep Sterling from dying? Or will all the young people move away, no matter what I do?''

Naomi reached out and took Deborah's hand. "Have you ever considered it might not be worth the effort?''

"Of course not. This is a wonderful town, with so much to offer. If it were only a little more economic, people would flock here.''

"And then the most wonderful things about it would be lost. You can't fight change, Debbie. Sometimes you have to accept.''

Deborah had watched acceptance all her life. People acted as if there were virtue in letting fate rule their lives. Whether a July thunderstorm ruined the hay, or all the children in a family ended up moving away, or a stroke victim didn't get emergency care, or the last gas station in town had to close. Take it on the chin.

Keep smiling. Life goes on. Well, others might get along fine with that kind of attitude, but she'd never managed to be very stoic.

If she believed in something, she couldn't just sit around wishing for it to come true. She'd work day and night to change desire into reality. She'd never give up until she succeeded. Like finding a doctor. How long had it taken to make that goal come true?

Again, the very thought of Bryant jolted her. He had too many commitments and obligations to ever make Sterling his permanent home. He'd finish his year and go back to Milwaukee and she'd have to begin her search again. She'd have to accept life without him. She lifted the mug halfway to her mouth, then set it back on the table so hard the salt- and pepper shakers rattled.

"I can't settle for the way things are, just because everyone else does."

Naomi's soft laugh brought a lump to Deborah's throat. "What's happened to upset you?"

Maybe it had been a mistake to come tonight, with her emotions so unsettled. Her mother understood her too well for comfort. "Nothing."

"If you don't want to talk about it, I understand, but I'll find out one way or another."

"From your spies, no doubt."

"What are grandchildren for?"

The twins would probably be by tomorrow. Deborah wondered how much they'd seen—and how they'd interpreted it.

"It's the doctor, isn't it?" Naomi probed.

"He'll be on crutches for a couple of weeks before they can put a walking heel on his cast."

"I'm not talking about his ankle."

Deborah signed. Of course not, that would be too easy.

"Have you fallen in love with him yet?"

"Mother!"

"If you haven't, you're a fool."

Words shouldn't have such power, but Naomi's acted like a wrecking ball, knocking a huge hole in the dam Deborah had built to contain her feelings. For days she'd been holding them inside, unable to tell the true ones from those created by stress.

"Matt believed it was his fault when Bryant fell," she said tightly. "It would have been easy for Bryant to let him take the blame. But watching Bryant ignore his pain and injuries in order to protect Matt, I thought I was in love with him then."

"And now?"

Deborah tapped the handle on the mug with her fingernails and struggled for the right words. "I loved Jay, Mom. Even after thirteen years, I still carry him in my heart. How could I love anyone else?"

"You love me. You love the twins. You love your brother and sister and their kids and all the people in this town."

"Romantic love is different."

When Naomi smiled, a subtle, sweet contentment filled her eyes. "You're right, it is. But let me tell you something you can't possibly know, since Jay died so young. Your father and I were married thirty years. During that time I fell in love with him over and over again, and each time it was with a different man. We both changed as we grew older, and sometimes those changes caused us a lot of stress, but in readjusting to each other, we found new things to love. If Jay had lived, you wouldn't love him the same way now that you did at seventeen. And you're not the same woman now you were then. If you love Bryant, it will have completely different aspects from loving Jay. Having loved Jay doesn't exclude loving Bryant."

Logically, Deborah wanted to believe her mother's words. It made perfect sense that every relationship didn't have to be the same. But even if she could believe she *had* fallen in love again, did she want to?

"After Jay died, I wasn't sure I'd ever be whole again."

"You amazed us all, the way you picked up the pieces so quickly."

"I did what I had to do, for the twins. I felt fragile for years, and I'm not sure I could ever face that kind of hurt again."

"If you do, you'll survive because you're strong."

Deborah stared at her hands, circling the mug until the images blurred into a mass of color. Jay's death had taken her by surprise. At twenty she'd been looking ahead to a full life, with no concept of how a trick of fate or a slick highway could destroy everything. Now she knew enough to temper the risks with caution.

"Bryant will leave next May, when his contract's up."

"So?"

Deborah shoved away from the table and paced the narrow length of the room and back. "He's leaving. Everything about being in Sterling is temporary to him. I'm not interested in temporary."

Naomi took Deborah's hand and urged her to sit back down. "*Life* is temporary, You know that better than most. Grab what joy you can and enjoy it while you can."

"And suffer when it's over? I don't think I can do that again."

"You can do anything. For years I've watched you beat incredible odds because you were willing to take risks. Why is this any different?"

"It just is. And I don't want to talk about it anymore." She didn't want to talk, or think, or feel. It was all still too new, too raw, and far too dangerous to her peace of mind. Maybe when she'd caught up on her sleep. Or maybe she wouldn't sleep again until Bryant went back where he belonged.

Bryant felt liberated. The walking cast gave him a lopsided gait, but it beat the hell out of crutches. He couldn't remember when two weeks had dragged by so slowly. The hall and doorways of his office had become an obstacle course. He hadn't been able to carry anything more cumbersome than a notebook. When his crutches fell out of reach, which they seemed to do at least a hundred times a day, he went through ridiculous gymnastics to recover then.

On the plus side, he'd become a lot more sympathetic to patients with mobility problems. And he'd relied on Matt a lot.

Slumping back in his office chair, he hefted his new cast onto his desk and admired it with a smile. Matt kept trying to compensate for what he believed to be his fault, and Bryant kept reassuring him it wasn't. But he couldn't stop savoring the change. If he'd known a broken ankle would give him his son, he'd have tried it months ago.

Of course, months ago the results wouldn't have been the same. It had taken a unique combination of circumstances, from that fateful kiss with Deborah, to

Matt's stealing a car, to attending the wilderness school. Without Deborah there at the beginning and the end, none of it would have happened. She deserved his deepest thanks.

He'd like to give her a lot more than that. He'd like to hold her in his arms again, plunge his hands into her glorious sun-kissed hair, drink in her wildflower scent.

He'd like to make love with her.

But he'd seen her only once since she brought him off the mountain. For some reason no one bothered to explain to him, she'd led Lodestone's next session. He thought she and Glen alternated during the summer, but she'd finished out their session and left with the twins again three days later.

She'd be home soon. He checked his watch. Any time now. He'd already asked Shirley to keep the next couple of hours open, so maybe he'd put his walking cast to good use and hobble down the hill to be at the Merc when she arrived.

By the time he'd made it halfway, he felt like a slave hauling twenty-ton stones to the pyramids. During the past two weeks, someone had doubled the length of Main Street. The blazing July sun cooked his skin and turned his white short-sleeved shirt into an oven. He reached the store covered with sweat and thirsty enough to drink a lake.

Pushing into the welcome air-conditioning, he felt as victorious as if he'd won the Iron Man. He bought a Coke and went through to the warehouse, where he intended to sit in the shade on the loading deck and drink it. And wait.

He knew Deborah would be surrounded by people, that she'd be tired and anxious to finish up the details of the session. He didn't care. He just wanted to see her. It seemed like a lifetime since they'd taken their midnight walk through the camp.

The lead truck came in just before four. Deborah backed up to the loading dock and started supervising before she hit the ground. Wisps of hair had come loose from her braid. High on the thigh of one pant leg, she had a smear of dried mud. The back of her T-shirt had been covered with autographs. She looked beautiful.

He knew the moment she spotted him. Pleasure flashed in her eyes and a smile tugged at her mouth until she could ease away to come and say hello.

"Bryant, what are you doing here?" She looked a little tired, but her voice held nothing but welcome.

"I missed you."

If he hadn't been so in tune with her, he'd have missed the break in her smile. But like a healthy heartbeat, it returned as steady and strong as ever. She made a show of noticing his new cast. "You're off crutches."

"The longest two weeks of my life."

Her laugh lilted above the din of unloading. "I'm sure. Look, it will take more than an hour to finish here. Maybe you and Matt would like to come over later? We could make ice cream or something."

"I'd rather take you to dinner."

She laughed again. "They might call it 'dinner' at the café, but everybody else in Sterling calls it 'supper.'"

"Nothing says we have to stay in Sterling."

This time her hesitation lasted long enough to tell him something. Unfortunately, he didn't know what.

"I'm going to have to pass," she said. "I need a long bath and a quiet evening. Maybe another time."

Even with his limited experience, Bryant knew a brush-off when he heard one. Maybe because of his limited experience, he had no intention of backing away. Not when fire raced through his veins and need filled his thoughts. "Okay. I'll dig out a bottle of good wine and be over later."

"Bryant, I'm—"

She broke off when one of the twins called from across the warehouse.

"Go, Deb. I know you're busy."

"Yes." She backed about ten feet away from him, letting their eyes stay locked. With each step, hers grew darker, and just before turning her tongue darted across her lower lip. Whatever troubled her, he knew the bond that had been growing between them for weeks still held.

He moved off to the side and leaned against one of the fifteen-foot-high sets of warehouse shelves jutting into the room. He'd give her time for a bath, but he wanted to see her before she tumbled into bed. Or maybe he could show up *just* as she tumbled into bed.

The session participants were still sorting out their personal gear and saying goodbye when Matt burst through the swinging doors. He paused for barely a second before yelling Deborah's name. He waved a big white envelope over his head and raced toward her.

She immediately went to meet him. Matt's dark blond head bent over Deborah's auburn one, then she threw her arms around his neck in a big hug. When he caught her around the waist and twirled her around, something wonderful burst in Bryant. Matt's miracle transformation showed in a thousand ways. Like showing affection and sharing happiness. His heart swelled at the picture of his son with the woman he loved.

He loved her. How had he not realized it before? She filled his thoughts, inhabited his dreams, colored his view of the future. Of course he loved her. He'd never been so happy as these months knowing her. Even before the change in Matt, she'd given him a level of inner peace he'd never known before.

Deborah broke free of Matt's arms, and to Bryant's surprise she pointed his way. She'd known he was still there without showing any indication of it. While attending to her work, a part of her had been aware of him. He understood how it worked. She had only to get within fifty feet of him for a subliminal radar to kick in.

Matt grabbed her hand and dragged her toward Bryant. Energy surrounded him. His eyes radiated excitement. He shoved the envelope in Bryant's face. "Dad. Look at this."

Barely a month ago, Matt had looked at him only with hate and anger, and the improvement still astonished Bryant. He put his arm around his son's shoulders and took the envelope. On top of it lay a certificate. Grand prize. Montana Youth Art Competition.

"I won a hundred dollars. Can you believe it, Dad? I won!"

Believe it? Bryant couldn't comprehend it. "I didn't know you'd entered."

"Isn't it wonderful?" Deborah gave Matt another little squeeze. "Not many people have talent like his. I'm so glad he decided to enter."

Awash in confusion, Bryant pulled his son into a hug. "Congratulations, son. I'm very proud of you."

The way their relationship had been before the trip to the mountains, Bryant could understand how Matt had kept something like this a secret. He'd probably be discovering new facets to his son for a long, long time.

But Deborah had known. Matt had confided in her. She'd managed to breach some of Matt's defenses in the spring, well before school let out for the summer. He met her eyes over Matt's shoulder and love swelled inside him. He probably owed her more than he'd ever know.

Matt broke away to look at the certificate again. "Do you think this means I have enough talent to be a real artist? I mean, like as a profession?"

"Of course it does," Deborah said.

Matt looked at Bryant, then dropped his eyes to the floor. "I don't think I want to be a doctor."

At the hesitation in his voice, Bryant wanted to cut away all the misapprehensions, to set the record straight once and for all. "I don't have a problem with that."

"You don't? I mean, everybody in your family is a doctor. Isn't that what it means to be a Conover?"

It had been for Bryant. And maybe if Matt had grown up within the circle of Conover doctors, he'd have accepted the same set of expectations. But these months away from Milwaukee had given Bryant a different perspective. "I want you to be whatever will make you happiest."

"Can I go to art school?"

"Absolutely. If that's what you want. When we go back home, we'll see about private lessons."

"Home?" Confusion flicked across Matt's expression, then he nodded. "Oh, yeah. You mean Milwaukee. I'm going to go show Lane and Ann, okay?" He sprinted off to find the twins, leaving Bryant staring into Deborah's eyes, with his words hanging in the air between them.

Home *was* Milwaukee. Matt might have forgotten, but Bryant couldn't. He had family there, a practice, his future. He'd come to Sterling to build a relationship with his son, and the next nine months could only strengthen what they'd begun. But when his contract ended in April, he'd go back to Conover Memorial and pick up where he left off.

Deborah's blue eyes seemed as clear and uncomplicated as Montana's sky. In them, he saw both strength and vulnerability. He'd fallen in love with her, but he wouldn't hurt her for the world. Thirty minutes earlier, he'd been on the brink of hurling them both into an abyss of potential heartbreak; now he saw clearly the chasm that stretched between them.

"I'd better get back to the office," he said. "I guess I should take Matt out to celebrate tonight, instead of coming to your place."

"He deserves it. Have a good time."

"Then I'll see you tomorrow."

"Sure."

He turned away without looking back. The nine months until April would be pure hell if he didn't find a way to stay friends with Deborah and forget he'd ever thought the word *love*.

Chapter Nine

Not a leaf had changed color, but the air smelled of fall. Deborah always marveled at how tearing a page off the calendar seemed to separate the seasons. She considered her annual Labor Day party a way of saying goodbye to summer.

Like the one she'd thrown to welcome Bryant and Matt, this was a cook-your-own kind of affair. She'd set up a long folding table for the potluck: baked beans, all kinds of salads, big wedges of watermelon and a wide selection of desserts. Nearly the whole town came, filling her yard from the house to the pond with games and laughter and goodwill.

She watched Matt swing out over the water on the rope and let go. When he landed with a splash that reached the bank, several girls squealed. He waded ashore and swept Lane into his arms, threatening to throw her in. Not for the first time, Deborah compared Lane's friendship with Matt to her own with

Jay, twenty years ago. And not for the first time, she wondered if she should be concerned. Not because she thought Matt might get Lane in trouble, but because he could break her heart when he left. She'd tried to bring up the subject with Lane, but Lane only laughed and claimed they were just friends.

Since *just friends* described her relationship with Bryant, Deborah didn't feel reassured. She emptied a bag of potato chips into a bowl and looked for Bryant. He and Glen sat in the shade in lawn chairs, with their legs stretched out. Bryant's cast looked the worse for wear, beaten up, covered with autographs, scarred and dusty. Glen held a sleeping Jason on his lap. Both men looked relaxed and content.

The summer had changed Bryant. As he and Matt became more and more like father and son, the mantle of worry he wore last spring had dropped away. His posture had relaxed and he smiled more. People in town accepted him; many had begun to talk about him as though he'd always be around.

Deborah knew she'd never find someone to replace him. Even if she managed to find another doctor, it wouldn't be the same.

With an impatient shake of her head, she crumpled the empty package and slammed it into a garbage can. *Many* of her friends had moved away. She'd always hated it, but she always survived. Why should this be any different?

Why should she be fretting about it this far in advance?

Because every day he meant more to her. There, she had admitted it. In spite of her mother's prodding, she still refused to put a name on it, but she cared about him—and dammit, she'd enjoy the friendship while it lasted.

Snagging two cans of soda from a washtub filled with ice, she took them to Bryant and Glen.

"What a woman." Glen popped the top on his and took a long swig. "You're wasted on those twins of yours."

She laughed and leaned against the tree trunk. "They appreciate me."

"Not the way a man would. Right, Doc?"

Bryant met her eyes over the top of his can and grinned. "Not all men know quality when they see it. Only us more enlightened types."

"True," Glen agreed. "Thank God. Otherwise she might have run off with some sweet-talking, low-thinking guy long before now. Some dude who only saw the surface beauty. And I can't imagine doing without her."

"If this is the way you talk about me when I'm here, I can just imagine the things you say when I'm not." Deborah pushed away from the tree and passed close to Glen to pull his cowboy hat down over his eyes. "Next time you can get your own drinks."

She'd made it less than halfway back to the table before Bryant caught up with her. "It's a great party."

She looked up at him with a smile. The rise of the walking heel on his cast made him look slightly off center, and a recurring tenderness filled her heart. She knew he saw his broken ankle as a testimony to his strengthening relationship with Matt. "Better than the last one you came to, probably."

"Definitely. Wanna come down and swing on the rope?"

"I don't think so. Not while the kids are in the water. I've been pulled off from below before, and believe me it's murder on the hands."

He took her hands and examined the palms. "No scars. Must have been a while ago."

She thought back, and a slow smile pulled at the corners of her mouth. "Oh, fifteen years or so." Jay had grabbed her ankle and she'd hit the water flat on her back. Then he'd dunked her, and when she came up sputtering, he'd kissed her. Treading water, she'd kissed him back and been surprised at the way his body felt wet and hard against hers. It had been fun then, exciting in a scary kind of way.

When Bryant's hand touched her cheek, she came back to the present with a start. He lowered his head, and she knew he intended to kiss her. Every instinct told her to let him, to enjoy, to respond.

Logic made her step away. Fifteen years ago, part of the excitement had been in not knowing the future. Now she knew exactly how the story would end, and happily ever after wasn't in the script.

Bryant hung up the phone and watched the rain drizzle down his office window. Lightning flashed far enough away that seconds elapsed before the thunder rumbled. Weather to suit his mood, nasty and unsettled.

Jeffery Lindstrom had had a heart attack over the weekend. This morning he'd had triple-bypass surgery. He'd take early retirement before the end of the month. And Dr. Matthew B. Conover, Sr., chief of staff at Conover Memorial expected Bryant to come home and step into Lindstrom's shoes.

It was the position Bryant had always wanted, ready and waiting. He felt like a condemned man, hearing he'd just gotten life with no parole.

Damn. He shoved away from the desk and paced a circle around it.

At least three times he'd explained to his grandfather that he had a contract to stay in Sterling until spring. Matthew, Sr. told him they could get a good lawyer. Bryant said there was such a thing as moral obligation. Matthew said previous commitment superseded anything else. Bryant said he didn't want to take Matt out of school. Matthew demanded to know why taking Matt out of school hadn't mattered last year.

Bryant hadn't mentioned Deborah.

When Shirley knocked on the door and handed him a patient chart, he went eagerly. Anything to take his mind off his thoughts, which were as circular as his pacing and about as productive.

He stitched up a gash across a farmer's palm and spent an extra ten minutes listening to how the man had sliced his hand open early that morning but hadn't dared stop working until the last hay had been stowed safely out of the weather. He tried to imagine the man then driving fifty miles in this storm to Bozeman, probably working a stick shift and coping without power steering.

By the time Bryant left the examination room, he felt more in a quandary than ever. The people of Sterling depended on him, but they'd gotten along without him before. They'd probably manage just fine again.

He spent the rest of the day weighing his options while he treated patients. Four sore throats, a bad case of sinusitis, one well-baby checkup and one new pregnancy case. By the time Shirley turned the lock on the front door, he felt as far from a decision as ever.

Shrugging into his jacket, he hobbled quickly through the rain to his car and drove the two blocks down to the Merc.

Deborah sat at the desk in her office tapping a pencil against her cheek. She didn't hear him approach until his foot hit the first step, then she whirled around in surprise with her hand at her throat.

"I didn't mean to startle you."

"No. I was just preoccupied. It must still be raining—you're all wet. Can I get you a cup of coffee?"

"Please." He took the chair at the end of her desk and watched her pour. Her hair fell loose around her shoulders, curling softly, inviting his fingers to weave through it. With the passing of summer, she'd traded her T-shirts for long sleeves. Her narrow waist and slender hips filled her snug jeans. He didn't know how he could leave her.

She put a mug on the desk at his elbow and sat down with her own. When their eyes met, she studied him silently for a moment. "What's the matter?" she asked softly.

Her insight made his heart jump. Had he ever known anyone who could read his emotions so easily? Had there ever been anyone who cared how he felt? He'd been looking for answers, but maybe he hadn't been asking the right questions.

"Is it Matt?"

He shook his head. "I got a call from my grandfather this morning. The current chief of family medicine at Con Memorial had heart surgery yesterday. He'll be retiring officially in a couple of weeks."

"I see." She left her chair to stand at the half wall overlooking the store. He heard the clatter of a shopping cart as it rolled down the linoleum floor, a couple of women laughed together, Charlie's voice called out to Ann. It all hummed in the background, while a progression of emotions worked across Deborah's profile. Finally, she turned to face him with a half smile, but he couldn't begin to guess the conclusions she'd come to.

"At least you accomplished what you came for. You and Matt are a family now."

Six months ago, he'd wanted nothing more. Now it wasn't enough. Not nearly. Now, his idea of family had expanded to wife and daughters, and until this minute he hadn't realized the extent to which his thinking had changed.

"So what are you going to do?" Deborah asked.

"Granddad wants me to come right home. I told him I was committed to stay until April."

"What happens if you don't go back now?"

"He threatened to hire someone else. I don't know whether he will or not. He might be trying to pressure me, but if I don't come to heel he could follow through."

"It's what you've always wanted."

"Yes."

She swallowed hard and forced a smile. "I won't stand in your way. I'll have to look for another doctor anyway. I just didn't expect it to be so soon."

He needed to touch her, to make a physical connection while establishing something more important but less substantial. He got up and took her hands. She lifted her clear blue eyes to his, and his sudden shortness of breath told him he'd finally gotten the right bead on which way to go. "There's another alternative."

Hope lit her eyes, as immediate and sure as any smile. "You'll stay?"

He pulled her closer against his chest. "You could marry me."

"Bryant, I—"

He kissed her. For weeks he'd ached to have her in his arms, to hold her close, to smell her scent and taste her lips. She held stiff for only a moment, then sighed an assent and melted against him. "I love you, Deborah. So does Matt."

"Oh, God." Abruptly, she twisted away with her hand to her mouth and turned her back to him. If she hadn't just kissed him with such generosity, he might feel rejected.

"Deb?" Gently, he pulled her around again. He lifted her chin and smiled down at her. "What is it?"

She drew a heavy breath and let it out slowly. "I thought I had everything under control. How I felt about you. How I knew you would leave."

"How *do* you feel about me?" he probed.

"I've loved you since summer, I think. Since that day on the avalanche when you were so wonderful with Matt." She sighed again and chewed her lower lip. "But I've fought it. Oh, God, how I've fought it."

"Why?" Resentment welled inside him. For weeks he'd been holding his own feelings back, waiting for some sign from her. And all those weeks her feelings had mirrored his. They could have spent the time together.

"Because I knew I'd lose you."

"That's why I want you to come with me."

"I can't. I have businesses here. Responsibilities."

That seemed like no reason to him. "Sell out. Charlie can buy the store and Glen can take over Lodestone."

"It's more than that. This is my place. It's where I belong. And there's my mother."

"Bring her to Milwaukee. She'd be better off there anyway." He didn't care what excuses she came up with, he'd find an answer for them.

She circled to the other side of her desk. She pulled out the chair, then shoved it back under with a crack of wood against wood.

"Look, I can't marry you. I'm sorry, I just can't."

If her reasons went beyond her roots or her family, they had to hark back to her past. He remembered the smile that had filled her eyes when she looked at her wedding photograph. He thought of all the times her husband's name had come up and how she'd refused to talk about him. "Because of Jay?"

Her spine stiffened and her chin came up. "What about Jay?"

"I don't know. Why don't you tell me."

She turned to the half wall and gripped the walnut railing that ran across the top. He watched the struggle for control. He saw the moment she decided to tell him, but she didn't turn around.

"Jay did everything vigorously." She spoke so softly he barely heard the words above the background din of the store. "Whether it was studying, working with his dad here at the Merc, playing football or riding his motorcycle. He loved life and made every minute count. We married right out of high school. In June. Nine months later the twins were born, and he loved them. Oh, he loved them so much. He used to carry them around with him. One in a carrier on his back and one in his arms. We took them everywhere, even backpacking. And life was good to us. When Jay's dad died of cancer that summer, Jay took over the store. It meant less time to play, but that didn't matter. We knew there was a season for everything.

"And then, just before the girls' first birthday, he rode his motorcycle into Bozeman on some errand. I don't remember what it was. He didn't start for home until late afternoon and by then it was raining. Barely a mile from home he skidded and ran into a tree.

"When I got there—" She stopped and closed her eyes. The color had drained from her face as though thirteen-year-old memories were as vivid as yesterday. "They airlifted him to Great Falls, but he died on the way. Everyone said having a local doctor wouldn't have made any difference. That his injuries were too extensive. I don't know."

Bryant rested his hands on her shoulders and brushed his lips across her hair. "What does this have to do with us? I love you."

"Don't you see? This isn't just for me. No matter how many times I fail, no matter how long it takes, I have to keep trying to bring a doctor to Sterling, so my friends and family can have the same access to care that you've always taken for granted. If I left, what would they do?

"All I've wanted since Jay's death was to make sure that kind of tragedy wouldn't happen again, to me or to someone else. I can't turn my back on my life here, any more than you can give up everything you've worked for in Milwaukee."

His hands framed her face. His lips captured hers. He poured every argument he had into the kiss. Words and habit seemed flimsy armor; he wanted the intensity of his love for her to strip it away. At her hesitant little moan, he wrapped her in his arms, promising shelter and safety and permanence with an embrace. They had so much, love and understanding and friendship. How could anything be more important than that? When he pulled away, her ragged breathing echoed his own.

"We can work it out," he said.

"You have to go back to Milwaukee."

"If you came with me, you'd never have to worry about it again."

Tears spilled down her cheeks and she brushed them impatiently away with the back of her hand. "I can't, Bryant. You know I can't."

"But you could let me go without you?"

"Oh, God, do you think it's easy?"

He swore and pivoted away. Maybe it wasn't easy, but he obviously didn't come very high on her priority list. "About as easy as stepping into the brink of hell."

"Please don't make it any harder."

"I couldn't possibly."

"When do you need to leave?"

As brusquely as he'd turned away from her, he swung back. He gripped her by the arms and drilled her with his eyes.

"I'm asking you one last time, Deborah. Come with me."

Tears still welled in her eyes, but she looked at him steadily enough. "You'll have new responsibilities. You'll be too busy to remember."

Did she think he could wipe the board clean with a change of scenery? Obviously she had no concept of how barren his life had been without her.

"That's your final answer?"

"Oh, Bryant, don't you see? The ties binding me to Sterling are at least as strong as the ones calling you home."

The discussion rose and fell around him. Bryant poured a cup of coffee and added sugar, carefully keeping his back to the others in the lounge. Many of these doctors had been at Conover Memorial when he'd first joined the staff. They were his friends, but since his return he felt as if he didn't know them at all.

Today's argument had obviously been raging for weeks, and he was trying to stay out of it. In his opinion, Conover Memorial needed a magnetic-resonant-imaging scanner as much as NASA needed an operating room on the moon.

This was a small hospital that had never been on the cutting edge of innovation. And since several other hospitals in the metropolitan area had them, what was the point? Prestige, perhaps.

Listening to the arguments, he found himself growing more and more angry. His little clinic in Sterling hadn't even had an X-ray machine. Of course, it wasn't his any more, so what difference did that make? For perhaps the thousandth time in a week, he wondered how long it would take Deborah to find another doctor.

For perhaps the millionth time, he wondered what he was doing back at Conover Memorial.

Matt had accepted the decision to return to Milwaukee without argument. Whatever Bryant wanted, he'd said. But his new closeness with his son had given him fresh insights. He knew Matt would have preferred to stay in Montana.

Two more doctors entered the lounge, reassuring themselves of the benefits of an MRI. Barely keeping his irritation hidden, Bryant tossed his disposable cup in the garbage and limped toward the door.

"Hey, Bryant, you can't run off yet. We could use your help on this."

Bryant turned and found the attention of the entire room centered on him. Damn.

Terrance White smiled, showing an exquisite row of perfect teeth. Terry was a neurologist who kept restating his position, as though everyone didn't know already where he stood. "A word from you to the chairman of the board might tip the scales. What do you say?"

Bryant smiled congenially. "You know my grandfather. Once his mind's made up..." He lifted his shoulder to indicate futility. "And since I'm not a member of the board, I don't have a vote."

"I'm sure you have some influence. If you proposed a few good arguments, he'd at least listen."

Bryant had worked with Terry for years, but the other doctor suddenly seemed too smooth, too hearty and too self-important. "I'm not sure I know any good arguments. I think I'll pass on this one."

John Anderson, a competent, respected heart surgeon, stepped closer. Like Terry, he had much to gain personally. "Now, Bryant, we all know your family *is* Conover Memorial. We know you love the hospital, and that you're as anxious as any of us to see that it takes its rightful place among the great medical institutions in the country. We have the talent here to put us on the map, but some of the equipment is antiquated."

John paused with a perfect sense of dramatic timing. Never letting his eyes wander from Bryant's face, he sipped at his coffee. "Your future is tied to this hospital. And the future of the hospital depends on progressive thinking."

Bryant knew that what he said next might influence his working relationship with these doctors for years. If he offended them, it would negate much of the good he could do in the future. If he appeared backward in his thinking, word would get back quickly to the board of directors. On the other hand, it might be interesting to say exactly what he thought and see the reaction.

Resisting the impulse, he managed a neutral smile and flipped his thumb into the good-luck sign. "I want what's best for Conover Memorial, but honestly, I don't have a vote. Sorry I can't stick around to discuss this. I'm running late for an appointment."

Behind him, because the pneumatic door closed so slowly, he heard John complain to whoever might be listening. "God, you'd think it'd kill him to put in a good word about this with the old man."

Bryant shrugged and glanced at his watch. If he took the stairs instead of waiting for the elevator, he could make it just in time.

He'd seen his grandfather only twice since his return. First at a family dinner, where Bryant had carefully avoided any one-on-one conversations with either his father or his grandfather. The second time had been in Matthew, Sr.'s office, where the older man had tried to reassure himself that Bryant had put his recent foolishness behind him and was ready to assume his new responsibilities.

His new responsibilities. Because Jeffery Lindstrom had retired so abruptly, Bryant's appointment as acting chief came the day of his return. He'd moved into his new office without making any effort to reestablish his old practice, and already piles of papers covered the top of his desk. Memos, budgets, schedules, applications, grant proposals. Lindstrom's secretary kept popping in to ask for decisions, and other department heads kept contacting him to determine whether continuity would be maintained.

Clearly, he'd made the jump into administration.

Matthew, Sr.'s secretary welcomed him with a smile. "He's expecting you, Doctor. You can go right in."

"Thanks."

The door of heavy carved maple opened soundlessly; the thick carpet silenced his footsteps. And Matthew looked up immediately.

"Come in, come in. Have a chair." The older man's bearing was as straight and commanding as ever, echoing the clarity and perception in his eyes. People who thought his age gave them an advantage soon learned otherwise. Only after working with him as a peer had Bryant stopped being intimidated. "How's your foot? When do you get that thing off? Are you getting settled in?"

With a sense of déjà vu, Bryant remembered how difficult his first couple of weeks in Sterling had been. He felt as much a stranger now.

"There's a lot to learn," he said. "I suspect it will take a while to adapt."

"Ah, yes. Undoubtedly."

Bryant waited a moment, allowing his grandfather to sit down first. He might often find the other man's domination frustrating or irritating, but he respected him, as a man, as a doctor and as the director of the hospital. The footsteps he'd chosen to follow were those of a giant.

The meeting took an hour, but it seemed twice that. As hard as he tried to concentrate on figures, projections and possible new directions, Bryant found it difficult to muster any serious interest. In the discussion about the MRI, he thought about how the other doctors kept trying to use him to influence his grandfather. When his grandfather talked about the importance of maintaining the family dynasty at the hospital, the goal he'd worked for all his life seemed superficial.

His thoughts kept wandering to his patients in Sterling, and how much he'd enjoyed treating them.

By the time his grandfather stood up, indicating they were through for now, Bryant knew the time for soul-searching had passed. He didn't want to spend the rest of his life shuffling papers. He wanted to work with people, long-range, on a continuing basis. He wanted to deliver babies and watch them grow into adults. He wanted to see new families begin and to deal with the elderly.

"I've changed my mind," he said abruptly, interrupting Matthew, Sr. in the middle of a sentence. "I don't want the position. I want to be a doctor, not an administrator."

The old man drew himself up to his still-impressive full height and glared at Bryant. "It's your birthright—you can't walk away from it."

"With all due respect, it would be my prison."

"We have no one else ready to step into Dr. Lindstrom's shoes."

"You'll find someone. I'm sorry, Granddad, I know you're disappointed—"

"Disappointed? I'm furious. You have an obligation—"

"To be true to myself. And I'm finally realizing what that means. I think I learned it from Matt."

"That boy—"

"Is a great kid, who knows what he wants out of life. I think I'll take the afternoon off and go ask his advice about the new shape my own goals seem to be taking."

Matthew, Sr. slapped the palm of his hand down on the desk. "I knew going to that town was a mistake. It twisted your thinking."

Grinning, Bryant backed toward the door. "Yes, I think it did. I'll let you know tonight what I've decided."

"Seven o'clock. Promptly."

"Mother, please. Be reasonable." Deborah stood across the quilt from Naomi, who continued to sew with such even stitches she obviously didn't feel a fraction of her daughter's concern. Growing more frustrated by the second, Deborah jammed her hands in her back pockets and barely refrained from stomping her foot.

"I haven't had a difficult day in weeks, dear," Naomi said calmly. "I simply cannot see why I should move in with you."

Because we don't have a doctor anymore. But Deborah didn't say that aloud. She'd been trying all week to not even think it. "But I worry about you."

"Yes, and I worry about you, too."

"Now that's nonsense." Unable to stand still, Deborah paced around the room. The quilt was nearly finished. Another day and it would be ready to take off the frames. Then a week of hand finishing the edges and the next one would begin. Naomi stopped sewing and pinned her needle carefully to the fabric so it wouldn't get lost. When she wheeled her chair around to face Deborah, her eyes were filled with such concern that Deborah turned sharply away to look out the window.

"Why did you let him go away?"

Leaning her forehead against the glass, Deborah suppressed a sigh. She hadn't cried, and she wouldn't. Nor would she let her perceptive mother know how much such self-restraint cost her. "He had to go. There was an emergency—"

"I already know the facts you've been passing around, Debbie. I also know that you've increased the pressure on me to move in with you so I can fill up those odd moments you can't occupy in any other way. Though heaven knows, you've been trying hard enough to make sure you have absolutely no free time."

"No!" Deborah swung back to confront such an accusation head-on. But the protest died in her throat. Perhaps her mother was right. But if she needed to avoid thinking, feeling, remembering, who could blame her? And since laughing was better that weeping, she let a small chuckle escape. "Well, maybe."

"So what are you going to do about it?"

"I'm going to come and box up your stuff and move you, in spite of your protests."

"That's *not* what I mean. What are you going to do about Bryant?"

"I've begun another letter-writing campaign. Somewhere, there's got to be a doctor willing to resettle here.

"That's not what I mean, either."

This time the sigh escaped before she could contain it. Not even when she was small had evasive tactics worked. She wondered why she kept trying.

"There's nothing *to* do, Mother. Bryant is gone, and I'm far too busy to worry about it."

"I guess there's no point in telling you you're a fool."

"None, whatsoever. I'd better get home. It looks like that monster storm they've been predicting has hit, and Ann hasn't been feeling well. But I really wish you'd give some serious thought to moving in with us. You know we'd love to have you."

"We'd all love it—for about a week. But I appreciate the invitation. Now hurry and beat the snow. They say we'll get a record amount for early October, so call me when you get home. I don't want to worry."

By the time Deborah got out to her car, she had to brush the windows off before she could drive. The heavy wet snow looked beautiful, held in the trees by their leaves, but it wouldn't take long before the limbs started to break under its weight.

Flipping on her lights and wipers, she was glad driving would take all her concentration. For a week now, she'd used every trick she knew to keep herself from thinking of Bryant. A mammoth preseason snowstorm ought to keep her mind occupied for a day or two.

Chapter Ten

Ann lay on the couch, pale and quiet and too listless to even watch TV.

Sitting beside her, Deborah smoothed back her hair. Ann's skin felt hot to the touch. "Is it too warm in here?"

"I just don't feel well."

"She's been kinda sick all morning." Sipping soda from the can, Lane plopped cross-legged on the floor beside them. "Like she was going to throw up. I asked her if she wanted anything to drink."

"Have you thrown up?" Deborah felt Ann's arms and back, but Lane had the wood stove going and the temperature in the room must have been close to eighty.

Ann shook her head.

"Lane, go get the thermometer."

A check of Ann's temperature indicated 101.4°, high enough for concern. Deborah made some weak

tea to settle Ann's stomach, and through the afternoon and evening she fought the fever. She used
sponge baths and alcohol packs and an over-the-
counter medication, and she referred to her house-
hold medical book for more suggestions.

Raising children by herself, she'd dealt with situations like this many times. Chicken pox, flu, colds,
strep. They'd had it, and she'd managed.

This time, she couldn't be stoical, not when the
medical book indicated Ann's symptoms might be
appendicitis and a snowstorm threatened to close the
highway to Bozeman. Frustration grew into anger at
the irony. A week ago she could have bundled Ann
into the car and taken her to see a doctor. Now she
faced the kind of dilemma she'd always dreaded.
Should she risk trying to make it through the mountains and end up freezing to death when they got
stranded? Or should she stay put and risk watching
Ann die if her appendix ruptured?

Damn Bryant.

He professed to love her, but he'd deserted her in
her hour of need. She washed Ann's forehead again
and prayed for a miracle. How dare he turn his back
on her?

About ten, she shook the thermometer and stuck it
under Ann's tongue again. She thought about turning on the radio, but Lane had gone to sleep curled in
a blanket on the floor. And what difference did it
make, anyway? Even if the roads were still open, she
wouldn't attempt them with a sick child.

She wondered how Bryant was spending his Saturday night. Maybe he'd decided to celebrate his return
to civilization with an evening at the symphony. Or

maybe he'd taken Matt to the movies. Or maybe they'd ordered in pizza. There must be a hundred possibilities in a city such as Milwaukee, which made it unlikely he'd be thinking of her. And even if he were, he couldn't know the agony of watching Ann grow sicker and sicker, unresponsive and unhappy. He couldn't know the fear of being stranded and feeling so damn helpless.

Ann moaned and curled onto her side with her arm cradling her stomach. Deborah went to the kitchen for some 7-Up and came back to kneel by Ann's side.

"Try to drink this, honey. It will make you feel better."

"I don't want it."

"I know. But have some anyway." She propped Ann up and tipped the glass to her mouth. Ann managed two swallows before closing her eyes and shaking her head. So much for plenty of fluids. It was going to be a long night.

Taking the glass back in the kitchen, Deborah started a pot of coffee and looked out the window while waiting for it to brew. Beautiful soft flakes swirled down, so close together they looked like lace. She imagined lace by the bolt, miles wide, being rolled out by a greedy customer to lay in giant folds on the ground.

When the power blinked out, taking all the lights, the lace outside turned whiter and brighter against the deep black night. Deborah felt her way to the table and lit one of the three oil lamps she'd gotten out earlier. With the wood stove she didn't have to worry about heat, and the water heater was gas. If Ann weren't sick and getting worse, they'd be fine.

She poured all the coffee that had perked into her mug and took the lamp into the living room. The soft light glinted back to her from the brass floor lamp and the picture frames on the mantel. Drawn by something she couldn't name, she went to the fireplace and picked up the old wedding photo of her and Jay.

They'd been so young. Naive and hopeful and careless. Never having experienced adversity, they'd known the future belonged to them. She touched Jay's miniature face, trailed her finger down his solid, youthful body and smiled.

Her mother was right. If she met Jay today, as he was then, she wouldn't be attracted to him. She wouldn't take him seriously. She might not even like him. Then, his recklessness had appealed to her; now, it would appall her. She had many good memories of him, but he was her past, not her future.

Her future lay in the two girls sleeping in the warmth of the wood-burning stove. She put down the photograph, aware that she'd just said a final goodbye to Jay. She wondered if she'd have given Bryant a different answer if she'd been able to do that long ago. Probably not. She'd rejected Bryant's proposal because he'd asked her to leave Sterling. Because she wanted to live in this isolated, snowed-in place with no electricity, no telephone and a sick child murmuring on the couch.

Suddenly Ann cried out. Deborah dropped onto the couch and gathered the girl into her arms.

"It hurts, Mom."

"I know, honey. I know. Would you like to try some more tea?"

"No."

"I can't give you more aspirin for another hour. But I'll sit here and hold you if you want."

"Okay. I wish Bryant hadn't gone. He'd know what to do, wouldn't he?"

"I'm sure of it."

She cuddled Ann closer and cursed Bryant under her breath. Why wasn't he here? How could some stupid obligation to his family's dynasty be more important than this? She'd tried so hard to guard against crises like this. Why did her failure have to come back and haunt her? Why did it have to be Ann?

Suddenly it didn't matter any more. Not Bryant. Not getting a doctor for Sterling. Not keeping her town from dying before her eyes.

She hated this place. The isolation and the lack of services and the hardship. Her mother was right. She should accept what she couldn't change and plan her life around reality. Realistically, Sterling would never be more than a shrinking flyspeck on the map, growing smaller with the exodus of each successive generation. She would never find a doctor.

And she would not continue to put her children in jeopardy. At first light tomorrow, she'd do whatever it took to get Ann to the hospital, and then she'd put the wheels in motion to move out of this godforsaken, dying, futile, wonderful place.

Maybe she'd go to Bryant, but maybe she wouldn't. She might move to Arizona, where the twins could live close to their cousins and where it never, never, never snowed. Maybe she wouldn't even let Bryant know she'd changed her mind about staying in Sterling. It

would depend on how mad she still was with him when
Ann got well again.

When the lights of a car turning into her driveway
played across her living room walls, Deborah bolted
to the window. Who would be out in this storm? Why?
Immediate concern for her mother filled her mind.
With the phones out, someone would have to come
instead of call, but how would Naomi have signaled
for help in the first place?

A heavy engine revved, and she recognized the dis-
tinctive roar of a Snowcat. Its lights lit the snow with
dazzling brilliance as it plowed up her driveway, and
fear for her mother turned to panic.

Seconds dragged on while she waited. The Snowcat
stopped at the corner of her porch long enough for
two figures to climb off, then pulled away. Obviously
it hadn't come to take her back to Naomi's. When her
visitors lumbered toward the door, she flung it open
before they could knock.

Not until they came into the glow of the lamp, did
she recognize Bryant and Matt under the caking of
snow. Her heart jerked, her head reeled. She grabbed
Bryant's hand to pull him into the room, and Matt
pushed the door shut behind them.

"You've come. Oh, my God, you're here. I've been
praying so hard. Quick, take off your wet things.
Ann's sick."

"How sick?" Bryant moved too slowly to suit her,
so she brushed his hands out of the way and popped
his coat buttons through their holes while he stood
stiffly and let her.

"What symptoms?"

"Nausea, fever, stomach cramps."

He shrugged out of the coat and tossed it at Matt. Going to the wood stove, he held his hands close to the lid. "If you've got something hot to drink, I'd really appreciate it."

Only then did she realize that even his voice sounded thick with the cold.

"How did you get here in this storm?"

Matt laughed and pulled the cap off his head, flinging snow and ice onto the floor. "By following a snowplow at ten miles an hour since the summit."

"But the roads are closed." She raced to the kitchen for a cup of coffee and thrust it at Bryant.

Grinning, Matt put his hands so close to the stove Deborah thought he might burn them. "At the Sterling turnoff the snowplow driver radioed in to the deputy, and he came and got us with the cat. It was great."

"We had to abandon the car." Bryant drank half the cup of coffee, then held the warm mug against his face.

When Ann woke up with a moan, Deborah hurried to sit beside her and looked at Bryant with tears blurring her vision. She'd needed him and he'd come.

"She started feeling sick this morning, and she's been getting worse ever since. I've tried everything to bring her fever down, but nothing's worked."

Bryant knelt beside her and touched the back of his fingers to her face. "Are my hands still too cold to touch her?"

They were. They felt like ice. "Maybe you'd better put them in water for a few minutes."

While Deborah dragged Bryant into the kitchen, Matt sat down by Ann. She heard Lane wake up and exclaim in surprise to find Matt there, then the murmur of all their voices faded while Bryant held his hands under a stream of lukewarm water. She had a hundred questions bubbling inside her. She had a hundred feelings aching to be expressed. Her concern for Ann overshadowed them all.

Bryant dried his hands and rolled up his sleeves before returning to Ann. He took her temperature again and examined her abdomen. When he finished, he pulled Deborah back into the kitchen.

With anxiety knotting her stomach, she tried to read his expression.

"It's appendicitis, isn't it?"

"Very likely."

His confirmation made fresh panic erupt inside her. When she tried to gulp it back, he pulled her into his arms.

"It's not all that serious yet, I promise. We should be able to stabilize her for a day or so. We might even be able to keep her from needing surgery."

With her hands on his upper arms, she drew back to look up at him. In the flickering lamplight, he looked tired and concerned, but happy, too.

"Thank you for coming back." She knew she meant for her own sake as well as Ann's, but that could wait.

All that night and into the next day, they tended Ann together. Lane hovered close until she could see for herself that Ann had started to improve, then she let Matt coax her outside. The snow stopped about midmorning, with fourteen inches in the valley and up to three feet at the higher elevations. The highway patrol said it would take another day to clear the road to Bozeman. The electricity came back on about noon.

As her fear for Ann ebbed, Deborah grew more conscious of Bryant. He seemed so at peace, so relaxed, so resolved. Watching him, a weird sense of expectation grew strong inside her, making it hard to sit still and harder still to get very close to him.

Sometime just before dusk, Lane and Matt burst through the back door, snow-covered and laughing.

"Mom, Matt said they came back so you could marry Bryant."

Deborah stopped stirring a skillet full of gravy and looked at Bryant. He'd been tearing lettuce into a bowl, but he set it aside and met her eyes.

Lane dipped her finger in the gravy and stuck it in her mouth. "If you do, will we live in Sterling or Milwaukee?"

"Milwaukee," she said.

"Sterling," he said.

Unsure she'd heard him right, she cleared her throat. "Last night before you came, I'd made up my mind to pull up stakes. Having Ann so sick scared me."

"During the past week, I realized I want to practice medicine where people are more important than balance sheets or the latest piece of sophisticated diagnostic equipment."

"So you gave up your dreams to come here."

"My dreams *are* here. It took me less than two days to discover I've lived my whole life by someone else's agenda. Sure, I could have been a top-notch administrator, but I'd rather be a damn good country doctor. It took a few more days to wrap things up, but I convinced the board of directors at Con Memorial to play big brother to a clinic here. We're going to update the facility and put me on-line to the computer network there."

Deborah's heart expanded in her chest until she couldn't breathe. Not in her wildest fantasies had she hoped for so much. "You're absolutely sure?"

"Absolutely. I love you, Deborah."

"Then just ask her, Dad. Stop procrastinating."

Bryant pushed the salad bowl farther onto the table and crossed the room. He took both her hands between both of his and brought them to his chest. His gray green eyes seemed silver bright, and his smile twisted the air out of her lungs.

"Deborah," he began. "Will you do me—"

"Wait!" Lane grabbed Deborah's arm and started pulling toward the living room. "You have to go where Ann can see, too."

Deborah laughed and Bryant shrugged, and they all went to stand by the couch, where Ann had been propped at an angle with half a dozen pillows.

"Okay, now," Lane said.

Bryant's eyes brimmed with laughter as he took Deborah's hands again. "Will you marry me?"

"I'd be honored."

Matt clapped Bryant on the back. Lane hugged Deborah around the waist. Ann laughed. "Hey, Doc. Welcome to Sterling. Again."

Deborah bent to kiss Ann, then found herself back in Bryant's arms. She smiled up at him, so full of this new love she wondered how she'd survived so long without it. "And may you have a lifetime of happiness in your new home."

* * * * *

Silhouette
ROMANCE™

COMING NEXT MONTH

#1048 ANYTHING FOR DANNY—Carla Cassidy
Under the Mistletoe—Fabulous Fathers
Danny Morgan had one wish this Christmas—to reunite his divorced parents. But Sherri and Luke Morgan needed more than their son's hopes to bring them together. They needed to rediscover their long-lost love.

#1049 TO WED AT CHRISTMAS—Helen R. Myers
Under the Mistletoe
Nothing could stop David Shepherd and Harmony Martin from falling in love—though their feuding families struggled to keep them apart. Would it take a miracle to get them married?

#1050 MISS SCROOGE—Toni Collins
Under the Mistletoe
"Bah, humbug" was all lonely Casey Tucker had to say about the holidays. But that was before handsome Gabe Wheeler gave her the most wonderful Christmas gift of all....

#1051 BELIEVING IN MIRACLES—Linda Varner
Under the Mistletoe—Mr. Right, Inc.
Andy Fulbright missed family life, and Honey Truman needed a father for her son. Their convenient marriage fulfilled their common needs, but would love fulfill their dreams?

#1052 A COWBOY FOR CHRISTMAS—Stella Bagwell
Under the Mistletoe
Spending the holidays with cowboy Chance Delacroix was a joy Lucinda Lambert knew couldn't last. She was a woman on the run, and leaving was the only way to keep Chance out of danger.

#1053 SURPRISE PACKAGE—Lynn Bulock
Under the Mistletoe
Miranda Dalton needed a miracle to save A Caring Place shelter. What she got was Jared Tarkett. What could a sexy drifter teach *her* about life, love and commitment?

MILLION DOLLAR SWEEPSTAKES (III)

No purchase necessary. To enter, follow the directions published. Method of entry may vary. For eligibility, entries must be received no later than March 31, 1996. No liability is assumed for printing errors, lost, late or misdirected entries. Odds of winning are determined by the number of eligible entries distributed and received. Prizewinners will be determined no later than June 30, 1996.

Sweepstakes open to residents of the U.S. (except Puerto Rico), Canada, Europe and Taiwan who are 18 years of age or older. All applicable laws and regulations apply. Sweepstakes offer void wherever prohibited by law. Values of all prizes are in U.S. currency. This sweepstakes is presented by Torstar Corp., its subsidiaries and affiliates, in conjunction with book, merchandise and/or product offerings. For a copy of the Official Rules send a self-addressed, stamped envelope (WA residents need not affix return postage) to: MILLION DOLLAR SWEEPSTAKES (III) Rules, P.O. Box 4573, Blair, NE 68009, USA.

EXTRA BONUS PRIZE DRAWING

No purchase necessary. The Extra Bonus Prize will be awarded in a random drawing to be conducted no later than 5/30/96 from among all entries received. To qualify, entries must be received by 3/31/96 and comply with published directions. Drawing open to residents of the U.S. (except Puerto Rico), Canada, Europe and Taiwan who are 18 years of age or older. All applicable laws and regulations apply; offer void wherever prohibited by law. Odds of winning are dependent upon number of eligibile entries received. Prize is valued in U.S. currency. The offer is presented by Torstar Corp., its subsidiaries and affiliates in conjunction with book, merchandise and/or product offering. For a copy of the Official Rules governing this sweepstakes, send a self-addressed, stamped envelope (WA residents need not affix return postage) to: Extra Bonus Prize Drawing Rules, P.O. Box 4590, Blair, NE 68009, USA.

SWP-S1194

JINGLE BELLS, WEDDING BELLS:
Silhouette's Christmas Collection for 1994

Christmas Wish List

*To beat the crowds at the malls and get the perfect present for *everyone,* even that snoopy Mrs. Smith next door!

*To get through the holiday parties without running my panty hose.

*To bake cookies, decorate the house and serve the perfect Christmas dinner—just like the women in all those magazines.

*To sit down, curl up and read my Silhouette Christmas stories!

Join *New York Times* bestselling author Nora Roberts, along with popular writers Barbara Boswell, Myrna Temte and Elizabeth August, as we celebrate the joys of Christmas—and the magic of marriage—with

JINGLE BELLS, WEDDING BELLS

Silhouette's Christmas Collection for 1994.

JBWB

HE'S MORE THAN A MAN,
HE'S ONE OF OUR

Fabulous Fathers

ANYTHING FOR DANNY
Carla Cassidy

Luke Morgan would do anything for his son, Danny. That's why he'd agreed to take a family vacation with his ex-wife, Sherri. Spending the holidays with his boy again was wonderful—and waking up next to Sherri again was giving him ideas. Luke would do anything for Danny, but could he risk his heart again?

Look for *Anything for Danny* by Carla Cassidy. Available in December.

Fall in love with our Fabulous Fathers!

Silhouette
R O M A N C E™

FF1294

Jilted!

Left at the altar, but not for long.

Why are these six couples
who have sworn off love
suddenly hearing wedding bells?

Find out in these scintillating books
by your favorite authors,
coming this November!

Come join the festivities when six handsome
hunks finally walk down the aisle...

only from

SILHOUETTE®

Desire®

JILT

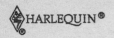 HARLEQUIN®  Silhouette®

The movie event of the season can be the reading event of the year!

Lights... The lights go on in October when CBS presents Harlequin/Silhouette Sunday Matinee Movies. These four movies are based on bestselling Harlequin and Silhouette novels.

Camera... As the cameras roll, be the first to read the original novels the movies are based on!

Action... Through this offer, you can have these books sent directly to you! Just fill in the order form below and you could be reading the books...before the movie!

48288-4	Treacherous Beauties by Cheryl Emerson		
		$3.99 U.S./$4.50 CAN.	☐
83305-9	Fantasy Man by Sharon Green		
		$3.99 U.S./$4.50 CAN.	☐
48289-2	A Change of Place by Tracy Sinclair		
		$3.99 U.S./$4.50CAN.	☐
83306-7	Another Woman by Margot Dalton		
		$3.99 U.S./$4.50 CAN.	☐

TOTAL AMOUNT	$	
POSTAGE & HANDLING	$	
($1.00 for one book, 50¢ for each additional)		
APPLICABLE TAXES*	$ _____	
<u>**TOTAL PAYABLE**</u>	$ _____	
(check or money order—please do not send cash)		

To order, complete this form and send it, along with a check or money order for the total above, payable to Harlequin Books, to: **In the U.S.:** 3010 Walden Avenue, P.O. Box 9047, Buffalo, NY 14269-9047; **In Canada:** P.O. Box 613, Fort Erie, Ontario, L2A 5X3.

Name: _____

Address: _____ City: _____

State/Prov.: _____ Zip/Postal Code: _____

*New York residents remit applicable sales taxes.
  Canadian residents remit applicable GST and provincial taxes.   CBSPR

"HOORAY FOR HOLLYWOOD" SWEEPSTAKES

HERE'S HOW THE SWEEPSTAKES WORKS

OFFICIAL RULES — NO PURCHASE NECESSARY

To enter, complete an Official Entry Form or hand print on a 3" x 5" card the words "HOORAY FOR HOLLYWOOD", your name and address and mail your entry in the pre-addressed envelope (if provided) or to: "Hooray for Hollywood" Sweepstakes, P.O. Box 9076, Buffalo, NY 14269-9076 or "Hooray for Hollywood" Sweepstakes, P.O. Box 637, Fort Erie, Ontario L2A 5X3. Entries must be sent via First Class Mail and be received no later than 12/31/94. No liability is assumed for lost, late or misdirected mail.

Winners will be selected in random drawings to be conducted no later than January 31, 1995 from all eligible entries received.

Grand Prize: A 7-day/6-night trip for 2 to Los Angeles, CA including round trip air transportation from commercial airport nearest winner's residence, accommodations at the Regent Beverly Wilshire Hotel, free rental car, and $1,000 spending money. (Approximate prize value which will vary dependent upon winner's residence: $5,400.00 U.S.); 500 Second Prizes: A pair of "Hollywood Star" sunglasses (prize value: $9.95 U.S. each). Winner selection is under the supervision of D.L. Blair, Inc., an independent judging organization, whose decisions are final. Grand Prize travelers must sign and return a release of liability prior to traveling. Trip must be taken by 2/1/96 and is subject to airline schedules and accommodations availability.

Sweepstakes offer is open to residents of the U.S. (except Puerto Rico) and Canada who are 18 years of age or older, except employees and immediate family members of Harlequin Enterprises, Ltd., its affiliates, subsidiaries, and all agencies, entities or persons connected with the use, marketing or conduct of this sweepstakes. All federal, state, provincial, municipal and local laws apply. Offer void wherever prohibited by law. Taxes and/or duties are the sole responsibility of the winners. Any litigation within the province of Quebec respecting the conduct and awarding of prizes may be submitted to the Regie des loteries et courses du Quebec. All prizes will be awarded; winners will be notified by mail. No substitution of prizes are permitted. Odds of winning are dependent upon the number of eligible entries received.

Potential grand prize winner must sign and return an Affidavit of Eligibility within 30 days of notification. In the event of non-compliance within this time period, prize may be awarded to an alternate winner. Prize notification returned as undeliverable may result in the awarding of prize to an alternate winner. By acceptance of their prize, winners consent to use of their names, photographs, or likenesses for purpose of advertising, trade and promotion on behalf of Harlequin Enterprises, Ltd., without further compensation unless prohibited by law. A Canadian winner must correctly answer an arithmetical skill-testing question in order to be awarded the prize.

For a list of winners (available after 2/28/95), send a separate stamped, self-addressed envelope to: Hooray for Hollywood Sweepstakes 3252 Winners, P.O. Box 4200, Blair, NE 68009.

CBSRLS

OFFICIAL ENTRY COUPON

"Hooray for Hollywood"
SWEEPSTAKES!

Yes, I'd love to win the Grand Prize — a vacation in Hollywood — or one of 500 pairs of "sunglasses of the stars"! Please enter me in the sweepstakes!

This entry must be received by December 31, 1994.
Winners will be notified by January 31, 1995.

Name _____

Address _____ Apt. _____

City _____

State/Prov. _____ Zip/Postal Code _____

Daytime phone number _____
(area code)

Mail all entries to: Hooray for Hollywood Sweepstakes,
P.O. Box 9076, Buffalo, NY 14269-9076.
In Canada, mail to: Hooray for Hollywood Sweepstakes,
P.O. Box 637, Fort Erie, ON L2A 5X3.

KCH

OFFICIAL ENTRY COUPON

"Hooray for Hollywood"
SWEEPSTAKES!

Yes, I'd love to win the Grand Prize — a vacation in Hollywood — or one of 500 pairs of "sunglasses of the stars"! Please enter me in the sweepstakes!

This entry must be received by December 31, 1994.
Winners will be notified by January 31, 1995.

Name _____

Address _____ Apt. _____

City _____

State/Prov. _____ Zip/Postal Code _____

Daytime phone number _____
(area code)

Mail all entries to: Hooray for Hollywood Sweepstakes,
P.O. Box 9076, Buffalo, NY 14269-9076.
In Canada, mail to: Hooray for Hollywood Sweepstakes,
P.O. Box 637, Fort Erie, ON L2A 5X3.

KCH